Unexpected Night

Thank you for your support

Thomas Long

Thomas Long

Copyright© 2020 THOMAS LONG

All rights reserved. This book or any portion thereof may not be reproduced without written permission from the publisher or used in any manner whatsoever without the written permission of the author or publisher except for the brief quotations in a review.
Printed in the United States of America
First printing, 2020

ISBN # 978-1-7354621-7-2

PUBLISHING SERVICES
provided by High Maintenance Publishing & Production, LLC

www.highmaintenance1.com

"Providing Opportunities, Inspiration and Education to Independent Writers."

Filmmaker|Publisher|Author *Celeste Celeste*
High Maintenance Publishing & Production, CEO

Prologue

It had to be about 3am when I finally pulled back into my yard. For some reason, I decided to drive down the side trail to the shed hidden in the middle of my 10-acre property, instead of pulling into the driveway like I usually do. I turned my headlights off and followed the natural light of the moon.

"A full moon! How fitting is that for a crazy night like this?" I said to myself as I shook my head.

About halfway to the shed, I started thinking about what had happened. I became so turned on, more turned on than I have been in my entire life. It was not a sexual turn on; it was something much more, something much stronger; something more intense. Even as I drove, the sensation completely took over my entire body. I felt my eyes slowly start to close. My body temperature started to slightly elevate. I could feel pressure being lifted off my shoulders. My lips suddenly became chapped, I realized my mouth was just as dry. I reached over to the center console and grabbed the bottle of water, only to realize it was empty as well. My heart rate increased. My stomach felt empty, I could just barely feel my legs, but at the same time, they felt so heavy. I slowed the car to a stop in the middle of the trail, slid it into park, and sat there idling as I relived the whole night. It was as if I was watching a movie in slow motion, frame by frame. Without realizing the time that had passed I put the car in drive again. I felt exhaustion and guilt start creeping in as I finally made it to the shed. When I arrived, I sat again for a minute as the tears filled my eyes and a smile began to form across my face.

Chapter 1

As I started to get out the car and stand up, I felt a slight relief that I was home safe. My thoughts were scrambled as the questions started getting louder in my head.

How could I have done this? How could I have been so careless? This cannot be happening to me. What do I do now? Do I call the police? I need to tell someone about this, I need help.

I walked over to a cabinet in the corner of the shed and pulled out a bag of weed. I sat there and rolled me a joint to calm my nerves before I walked back home. I started thinking about how this night began...I started off at a low-key jazz lounge.

I pulled up to this gorgeous, well-lit, free-standing 3-story building. The parking lot was half filled with some of the most beautiful cars and trucks. I pulled my all-black Dodge Charger Hellcat up to the valet parking. Once the attendee walked to my driver side, I opened the door and got out. I could see the youthful smile and him nodding his head high in approval.

"Sir, please excuse my French, but that's a bad ass car," he said.

I always love when people lust over my girl. I looked at him smiled and said, "Yes, thank you, she's a good girl. You can take it around the block for a spin, just be careful."

He looked at me, laughed, and said, "Yeah right...I wish. I can't even afford to put a full tank of gas in there."

As the valet hopped into the car, I replied, "Okay young man, it's your call, but if you change your mind just be careful please."

I started walking toward the building and heard my car engine come to life. I stopped and turned to look back; that kid had the biggest smile on his face. He looked at me and gave me a thumbs up, so I smiled back and gave him a nod in approval. I turned and started down the long pathway leading to the building.

Once I entered the building, I asked the young woman at the entrance to point me toward the bathroom, where I went straight to the mirror for a few last second adjustments to my slim-fitted black suit. I looked in the mirror and smiled back at my perfect reflection, as I thought to myself, *Damn boy, you look right.* I turned and walked out of the bathroom, making my way to the jazz lounge. I instantly spotted the most beautiful woman I have ever laid eyes on. I gave her a quick smile as I made a beeline to a small table toward the back of the room. Every few steps I would glance over in her direction to see if she was looking at me and to my pure delight; she was.

I sat down and tried to redirect my attention to the band on stage, but that was short lived. I could not keep my eyes off of her. I saw that her eyes were filled with just as much lust as I had in my own.

She stood up from her table and headed towards the back exit, but I was in her direct path. She was no taller than 5'5" with her heels on. She had thick, curly jet-black hair with a slight angel's breath of light brown highlights, perfectly placed by God himself. Her eyes were light brown and could penetrate the soul of the most hardened person. She wore a tight, beautiful blood red dress that came down about six inches above her knee, but you could only see a small portion of her perfect brown skin, because of the sexiest thigh-high, high-heeled boots. With every step she took toward me, my body temperature went up one degree. There was no one else in this building that I wanted. As she walked to me, our eyes locked and neither of us looked away. My palms started to sweat; my mouth suddenly became dry. She was about 10 feet away from me and I decided that I was going to speak to her. This might be my only chance. Now she was 5 feet away, and it felt as though it was only her and I in this whole place.

"Excuse me sir; sir, excuse me. Can I get you something to drink?" a waiter asked.

In that moment, I was brought back to reality, and she swiftly and gracefully walked past me towards the bathroom. At first, I looked at the waiter like he did something wrong, but then started to smile to myself.

"Yes, sir can I please have a double of crown apple and a splash of Sprite please, and a glass of water," I said.

When the waiter returned, he asked if I wanted to order food at that time, but I passed on the food for now.
As he was walking away, I saw her returning from the bathroom, heading right towards me. She placed her hand lightly on my shoulder; I reached up to touch her perfect skin, just as I did, she slipped me a note.

Meet me at…

I started to shake my head with a slight grin on my face as I thought to myself, *damn she is beautiful.*

I sat back in the corner, next to the cupboard, and lit the joint I had just rolled, while I continued to shake my head over and over. Once I was almost done with the joint, I rolled a second one and stood up to smoke the rest on my way back to my house. I exited the shed and slowly started my commute. As soon as my back-porch light started to come into my view, I dropped the joint on the ground and lit the second one. I took about five more steps and looked up at the full moon, thinking about how stupid I could be sometimes. A single tear started to fall from my left eye, but I quickly wiped it off.

I continued walking down the trail until I reached the stairs to my porch. I turned to the right and walked over to my rocking chair to sit and collect my thoughts. I needed to stare off into the distance and think about what had just transpired over the last five hours. I ended up sitting on the back porch for hours until the sun began to rise. I realized I had not slept at all last night, so I decided to go into the house and try to fall asleep. Instead, I found myself just lying in my bed staring at the ceiling.

Sleep was apparently not going to come to me anytime soon, so I finally gave in, got back out of bed, and turned on the TV. It just so happened that the first thing that popped on the screen was the local morning news. They were covering a story about a young lady that was the victim of a murder, dramatically explaining that the cause of death was presumed to be strangulation. I could not hold it in any longer; the tears started flowing down my face. My emotions were getting the best of me and I could no longer control them. Before I could change the channel, there was another news alert, this time about 3 people killed in a drive-by shooting; amongst the victims was a young girl who was walking by and was hit in the chest twice. I walked into my bathroom, opened the medicine cabinet, and grabbed a bottle of muscle relaxer. I took three of them. The world was such a horrible place.

I walked back into the living room to roll another joint, I needed help to relax and get some sleep. Finally, the weed and pills join forces and worked their magic, 45 minutes later I was in a deep sleep.

I thought I must have slept for 24 hours, because when I finally woke up, the sun was coming up again. I reached over and grabbed my phone. I had missed 100 calls and 75 text messages. I finally checked the date and time and saw it was Monday morning. *Wait...did I just sleep for a full two days?* Before I could collect my thoughts there was a loud banging on my front door.

"Thomas, are you in there? Open the door! Thomas, open the door," I heard someone yelling.

"Yea! Hold on, I'm coming, dammit. The hell are you banging on the door like the fucking police?" I yelled back.

"Where the hell have you been? What happened to you? Why haven't you called me back? Why haven't you text me back? Are you okay? Are you going to answer me Thomas?" she said, with her voice cracking.

I opened the door and stood there, waiting for a second, before I responded with,
"Are you done? Would you like to write that down so I can answer your thousands of questions? If you must know, Michelle, I have been sick as a dog and on top of that, I have had the worst headache. I could barely open my eyes."

She said with a softer voice, "Did you go to the ER or the doctor?"

I said to her, "Come on, you know me, I hate those places. I just took care of myself. I'm a big boy; I can take care of me. I turned my phone off and forgot to turn it back on."

"So, you were sick all weekend."

"Yes, I was."

"And you took care of yourself?"

"Yes, I did."

"No one came over to help?"

"Nope I did it all by myself. Girl, I'm grown. I can take care of myself."

Michelle silently stared at me for a few seconds, but I could see in her face that she wasn't buying what I was selling. She's my best friend and knows me better than anyone. I was already a bad liar as it is, but this lie was doomed the moment I started to tell it.

After staring me down, she looked me directly in the eyes and said, "You are such a fucking liar. You are going to actually sit here and tell me that bull-shit story that you were sick, and you took care of yourself? When you are sick, you are the biggest baby I know. Are you forgetting we were roommates for like…7 years, and if you so much as get anything in your eye you act like the world is coming to an end? Now, are you going to tell me the truth about why you were missing the pass few days?"

"What the hell? Why would I lie about being sick, dammit?"
"I don't know, Thomas! Why *would* you lie about getting sick?"

"Girl, you tripping!" I turned away, in part for effect, in part to hide my face as I tried to gather my thoughts and figure out what to say next. I knew she was not going to let this go without a fight.

"You're also the worst liar I have ever met. But you know what? I am going to give you credit for trying to pull that one off. I cannot believe you actually had the balls to say that you were sick, but that isn't even the funny part, you tried to say you took care of yourself."

"What's so funny about it? I been single for years, who the hell you think took care of me all those years? Nobody! Thank you."

"Who the hell do I think did it? I don't have to think on this one, I know exactly who did because it was me! I took care of you when you got sick, because you would cry like a 2-year-old little girl."

"Shit, okay…whatever. Do you really want to know? Just promise me that you will never tell anyone about this."

"Promise!"

I knew I could tell her what happened without her passing any judgement or telling someone else. We have had many conversations before that made be believe she would freak out on me, but…here she is again. So, I took a deep breath.

"Well, you might want to sit down for this because you won't believe it." I briefly paused and took another breath. "So, Friday night I went to this nice jazz lounge. I met this female, and damn she was fine."

"A female was involved. I'm shocked."

"Damn, girl do you want me to tell you or no? Anyway, I was at this jazz lounge and the most beautiful female I have ever seen slipped me a note. So, I met up with her for few too many drinks after the lounge."

After about an hour of me telling her this long story, I stood up and walked to the kitchen to get a beer. I popped the beer open and said to her, "Are you okay?"

She just looked at me, stood up, turned around, and walked out without saying a word. She didn't even ask me a question about that night. She didn't even cry. I saw no emotion from her. She just turned and walked out the house without speaking a word. This had me worried, but I trusted her, and I figured she just needed time to process what I just told her.

Chapter 2

It had been a few days since I told Michelle about my night, and still had not hear from her. I sat down and texted her to ask if she wanted to go out for a few drinks, but I never got a return text. I was starting to think I have made a wrong decision by telling her, but I had to trust her. I trust very few people and she was probably at the top of that short list.

I put the phone down on my knee and lit a joint I had rolled earlier. I picked the phone up again and started to text a few different chicks to see if I could set up something for the night. I scrolled down my contacts list and came across a number that didn't have a name attached to it, but when I pulled up the text history it was a short conversation about a Dom/Sub relationship. I looked at the time of the last message and it was time stamped more than a year ago, on March 13th. Why would I not continue this conversation considering this is something I have been wanting to explore more? I replied back to the last message, saying hello and giving the background; I was looking through my phone, saw the last message, but I hadn't saved the number and just wanted to see who it was.

Not even two minutes passed before I received a return text.

"Hello Thomas! Long time! Looks like I ran you off since we last spoke," the unknown texter replied.

"LOL…To be honest I have no clue who this is."

"Guess I wasn't what you were looking for."

"I don't even know who you are. But if you won't tell me I won't beg you."

"LOL… This is Shannon! Do you remember me now?"

"Ohhhhhh yesss….Damn girl how have you been? What's new with you?"

"I'm doing well. Thanks for asking. So, do you remember what we were talking about the last time we spoke to each other?"

"No, I do not remember at all, sorry. Will you refresh my memory?"

"We were talking about BDSM, the Dom/Sub relationship. You said you wanted to maybe explore that more in-depth. Are you still interested in that type of play?"

"I actually have thought about it a lot the pass few days."

"What about this lifestyle that piques your interest so much? Reason I ask is this life is not for most people. It is built of extreme trust and more importantly to know your sub's body and limits. But you also need to know when to push those limits and knowing when not to. So have you done any research on it, and if you have, what category do you feel like you fall into?"

"I have always been the more aggressive one in bed. I enjoy the choking, smacking, and dirty talk. So, I would say I'm more of the Dom type."

"Well, to be honest, because you are rough in bed doesn't make you a Dom. Begin aggressive in bed only makes you aggressive in bed, but we can always talk about that more in depth at another time. When are you available to meet?" She asked.

"Tonight is good."

"8 tonight, there's a bar close to my house. I'll text you the address."

"Make it 9pm tonight."

"Perfect! I will send you the address when I get home. I look forward to meeting you Sir."

"Okay! See you then."

I put the phone on the arm of the couch, stood up, and walked into the kitchen. It was still early in the day, so I knew I had enough time to hit the gym and have dinner at my place before heading over to meet her. I got over to the freezer, grabbed a slab of ribs out, and started to prep the meat for my smoker. I knew it would be ready in a few hours, long before I had to meet up with this chick.

After I got dinner started, I went to my room and changed clothes so I could go to the gym for an hour or two. Once in the gym parking lot, I got out and opened the trunk of my car to pull out my bag with my workout gear in it. I turned and saw a tall, beautiful slim female out the corner of my eye. She looked like she just finished an intense work out; I waved and smiled at her, and she returned the gesture.

I walked into the gym and it smelled like a sweaty icebox. *Damn, I love that smell*, I said to myself. It was the true smell of hard work.

As I walked in I saw the front desk woman I flirted with from time to time, but she was married, so I was never expecting anything but a little flirting. I walked past her as she waved me over to her desk.

"Hey Thomas. How have you been?" she said in a low tone.

"What's up Mindy? Looking good as always I see! How's your day going?" I said through a smile.

"I'm good just working as always. Another day another dollar," she said.

"Got anything fun planned for this week?" I asked.
"Nope just clean my house with no clothes on and enjoying my alone time. My husband is taking the kids for the weekend so I can relax a little. Lord knows I needed this more than anything right now. Well, maybe a little chocolate too." she said with a devilish grin.

I smiled and said, "I'll be at the bar across the street tomorrow, around 10pm. If you like, you can join me and grab a few drinks. But listen sexiness, I have to go get this workout in, I gotta find my sexy again."

"From where I'm standing you never lost it," she said to me.

"Now you got me blushing," I said smiling at her.

"Oh yeah, you're blushing. Ha! Okay, handsome, have a great workout," she said as she turned toward the computer screen.

I put on my ear buds and turned up the music to get into the mental space needed to get this work in. I just thought to myself as I walked over to the stationary bike, *Damn, if I ever get the chance to get my hands on her, I'm going to put in some major work.*

I dropped my bag on the ground next to the bike, pulled out my bottle water, rag, and turned up my trap music. An hour and a half later I stepped off the bike and I could feel all 20 miles. My legs shook a little, but I walked over to the free weights and for the next hour put myself through an intense full body workout. Once I finished my last rep, I walked to the bathroom and did what everyone does after a great workout…I took about 5 good selfies.

As I walked toward the front door, I saw Mindy again, she was sitting at that front desk looking like the hottest science teacher I had ever seen. She looked up at me and waved goodbye. I waved back and returned the smile.

When I got to my car I popped the trunk and threw my bag in the back. I got in and started to back up when I noticed a folded piece of paper on the windshield. I put the car in park and got out to grab the note, placing it on the center console, I reached up and opened the sun visor, grabbing and lighting the joint I had before pulling off. My drive home was only about 15 minutes.

I pulled back into the driveway and when I stepped out of my car, I could smell the ribs cooking. Dammit, I was getting hungrier and hungrier with every step toward the house. Once I opened the door it was better than I thought and the smells made me forget, temporarily, about the note. I walked to the kitchen and made me a nice size plate, sat down at the island in my oversized kitchen, and turned on the local news.

They were still looking for the person who killed that lady in the warehouse district. This was getting a lot of airtime; she must have been someone really important. I just shook my head and finished my meal.

After eating I cleaned up my mess and did a quick scan to make sure I did not miss anything. While looking around my home I thought to myself, how blessed I was for the things I had, and how I would kill to keep everything I earned over the years.

I was brought back to the moment when my phone's notification sound buzzed with a text from Shannon. She sent the bar's address, where I was supposed to meet her. It was about 45 mins away and it was already 7pm, so I had to get a move on it.

I walked to the bathroom and turned the shower on, then I grabbed my phone off the sink to play some music, and shave. Music can always get me into the right mindset, no matter what mood I need to get in or out of. When I finished shaving the whole bathroom and mirror was steamed up; I jumped into the shower to get fresh and clean for the night ahead of me.

When I was done and ready to walk out the door I texted her saying that I was about to get on the road and head to the bar. I got in my car, adjusted the radio, and made myself comfortable for the drive. That is when I realized that I never looked at the note that I found on my windshield.
When I opened it read: *Hello! I know this is a little odd, but I saw you walking into the gym and you caught my attention. You should give me a call. I would love to meet you out for few drinks and get to know you. My number is 407-953-07...oh and BTW my name is Jennifer.*

Chapter 3

As I pulled up to the parking lot, I could see that there were not many people inside the bar, and that was perfect for the night. I was not in the mood to be around too many people. I walked through the door and the smell of smoke pushed me back a few feet. Once I regained my bearings, I walked in and sat at the corner of the bar, pulling out my phone to text Shannon that I was there and waiting. She replied right away that she was walking into the door.

When she walked in, she was wearing a pair of black, six-inch heels with silver spikes covering the shoe. Her legs were in amazing shape; looked like she had never missed leg day in the gym. In fact, it looked like she worked her legs out daily. With every step you could see the power in her legs. Her dress was a tight, little black dress, which showed off her perfectly round ass and beautiful breasts, displaying as much cleavage as the dress allowed. Her eyes were a deep, flawless hazel brown; they were almost a golden color. She looked up and saw me in the corner and smiled. Her teeth were as white as snowflakes and her smile could light up a dark room; and it did. Her hair was thick and black with very tight curls.

Once she sat down, she stared at me for about 5 or 6 seconds before she said anything.

"Well Mr. Thomas it's great to finally meet you," she said with a smile.

"This isn't the first time we met. I do remember you woman," I said jokingly

"Well it's been so long it might as well be. You know what...hold on a second," she said with a grin.

She stood up and walked about 20 feet away and turn back around and started walking back toward me.

"Hello handsome! How are you? My name is Shannon. What's your name?" she said.

I responded back, "Hello Shannon! Pleasure to meet you. My name is Thomas. Would you like to have a seat and have a drink with me?"

"I don't know, I'm meeting someone up here."

"Are you sure? I don't think he's as cute as I am," I said between laughs.

"No, he definitely isn't as cute as you are. Fuck it. You can't get mad at a girl for upgrading, right? So, yeah, you can get me that drink" she said.

I asked, "So how have you been? Are you married, on lockdown, got a crazy ex, or anything?"

"No, I will never get married! Honestly, it is not intended for someone to be with just one person. So, with me I am considered a sub, or submissive, to my Dom. My pleasure is only to please him in every way he desires. I do have limits. For one, when or if we ever play, you have to leave the phone in the kitchen. Two, nothing illegal. Third, and most importantly, always wear protection, and that is for both yours and my safety. Those rules are not to be broken, ever. Other than that, I'm there to serve my Dom," she said.

"So, you are saying that you would give the freedom to do whatever I want or wanted to try sexually?" I asked in disbelief.

"Yes, but I do warn you that I like it hard, and as deep as you can. To be honest, I always wanted to try to DP with two big black cocks, but you would never believe how hard is it to get two guys to come fuck me at the same time. I thought it would be much easier than this."

"Oh, it's pretty hard to get two guys to come fuck one chick at the same time without them knowing each other. Shit, it's hard to get two guys that know each other to come do it," I said.

"So, are you more dominate or submissive? I am fairly sure you are more of a Dom, because I have rarely seen a black man as a sub. Now, I am not saying I have never seen a black sub, but the majority of black men are very dominating," she said to me.

"I am dominant in the bedroom. But I also make sure what I am doing is pleasurable to my partner. I know I am not a sub in any type of way."

We sat at the bar for the next few hours talking, flirting, and a little touching. The topic of conversation was wide ranging, from books, to politics, to sports, and do's and don'ts in the bedroom. It was crazy to me because she only had a few don'ts. No cameras and always condoms, but other than that, I had no limitation on what I could and should do to her.
She also explained that her first Dom had trained her very well, even though we didn't get too far into her training with him. About 1:30 a.m. she asked if I would like to go back to her place and play. I looked over at the bartender and asked for the check.

After I paid the check, we stood and walked outside. She looked over at me and told me to follow her, and that she only lived 5 minutes away. I got in my car and pulled up behind her at the stop light. The drive was short. We pulled up to an apartment complex that was well lit and had a key card only entrance. Once we came into the apartment complex and parked in front of her place, we made our way to her condo on the second floor.

We were about five feet inside of her place when she turned to me and asked, "Do you know why I love my place?"

I just stood there and looked at her. So, I replied, "No sweetheart, I do not."

"Well, because no one lives above me, under me, or on any side of me. The apartment across the hall is even empty. Which means you can fuck me as hard as you want," she said with a devilish grin on her face.

And without another word said she dropped to her knees and pulled out my hard cock. Once she had my pants off, she looked at my tool and her eyes widened as she licked her lips and tilted her head back at me and asked, "How big?"

I smiled at her and said, "Almost 10."

"Yummy! Can I suck your cock, Sir?" she asked me.

Without saying anything, I nodded my head to let her know that I approved of her request. She took a deep breath and started sucking my cock as if it was her lifeline. The more she sucked, the harder I got. The harder I got, the deeper and more forceful she became with taking as much as she could. I grabbed the back of her head and thrusted my harden manhood deeper than she could take. She started to push away, but I pulled her back. I could see her eyes start to roll behind her head. I pulled my cock out of her mouth as I watched her gasp for air.

She looked up at me, I noticed her eyeliner was running down her face. Her eyes were red but filled with so much lust and hunger.

"Thank you, Sir. Thank you! Can I please have more of your co…"

Before she could finish her words, my dick was back down her throat. I grabbed the side of her head and started to fuck her face as if it was her pussy. She was dripping saliva down her chin. My nuts were soaking wet. I pulled her up to her knees, turned her around, bent her over the kitchen counter, spread her legs open, and started to lick her pussy from as well as her ass. With every lick I could feel her knees shake.

I licked my finger and slid two of them inside of her. She was soaking wet! I could feel her juices running down my hands and down my arm. I leaned over licked the juice off my arm. With my other hand I reached up and pushed her back down to let her know that I wanted and needed more access to her, she followed my lead. She leaned forward and arched her back downward, which gave me direct access to her ass. I pulled my fingers out of her pussy and spread her ass cheeks as I entered her with my tongue.

"Don't Stop!" She yelled out in pleasure.

I started fingering her wet pussy again, until I could feel her dripping again, then I stood up and lead her to the bedroom. I turned her around and started to kiss her deeply. I pushed her back against the wall and whispered in her ear, "Drop to your knees and swallow me."

As she started sucking my cock I looked to my left and saw arms and leg restraints. I reached over and grabbed the arm restraints and applied them to her wrists and clipped them together so I could control both arms. I pulled her arms up over her head and braced them.

"Open your mouth." I demanded.

She began slowly sucking my cock, taking it deep. Every time my cock hit the back of her throat her eyes watered more and more. I slowly started dipping my manhood in and out of her mouth; I was going deeper and faster fucking her mouth. I pulled my cock out of her and looked down.

"Thank you, Sir!" She said with the biggest smile on her face between deep breaths.

I reached down and pulled her up by her hair and bent her over the edge of her bed. I grabbed the condom and pulled it on with joy, knowing that this is going to be good.

I rubbed her pussy to make sure it was ready for me to enter. She was soaking wet with anticipation. When I pulled my glazed finger out of her pussy, I brought them right up to my face! They tasted just as good as they looked. I slowly guided half of my 10-inch cock inside of her, pumping in and out slowly while rotating my hips in a circular motion. Every few minutes I would go deeper and deeper. The deeper I would get the louder her moans would grow. The louder she got the faster and harder I would go until I was fucking her so hard, she was screaming.

To be honest I did not know if it was pleasure or pain, but I was not going to stop because she never used her safe word. I slowed down to a deep grinding rotation, then I made her crawl onto the middle of the bed and pushed down on her back between her shoulder blades causing her to lay flat on the bed. I slightly lifted her hips and spread her legs. When I climbed on the bed I had full unrestricted access to her.

I slowly inserted the tip the I picked up the pace and become much more aggressive until I was pounding her as hard as I could for a solid 10 minutes. Halfway into it she looked back at me, her makeup was a mess and she had tears in her eyes. I knew she was about to cum again because her eyes begun to roll, she dropped her head to the bed while gripping the bedsheets tight with both hands. Somehow, she arched her back lower. I went deeper, feeling my nuts smacking on her pussy.

She was trembling with pleasure.

"Fuck! I'm about to cum again." She screamed.

I stopped pounding on her and eased my dick as deep inside of her as I could. Once I knew I was as deep as I could get, I started grinding. I could feel her cumming, her pussy was getting tighter around my dick. She started to shake uncontrollably. I pulled out of her and flipped her onto her back and slipped back inside her.

Her legs were wrapped around my waist and I went back to work, pounding her as deep as I could. The deeper I went inside of her, the deeper her nails dug into my back. The slight pain of her nails turned me on more. I went faster…deeper. I could feel her juices squirting out all over me.

She yelled out, "Thomas I'm still cumming. Oh my God, I cannot stop cumming. What the fuck are you doing to me? You are hitting something inside of me…I'm cumming so much. Please don't stop…please don't."

I didn't want to stop fucking her. It was just so good, but I had stop I could hardly breathe. I slowed down to long deep strokes. I could still feel her cumming. I looked into her eyes to watch. I quickly pulled out of her and it sent her into another world. I felt her cum squirting onto my stomach. I moved to the side and finger fucked her as fast as I could until I saw her explode all over the room.

I felt her entire body go limp as I collapsed on the bed. I pulled my fingers out of her and licked them, then I melted onto the bed. All I could think was how fucking hot that was. I looked over and she was already sleep.

I just laid there until I was able to get up and shower. Once I was done I got dressed and left. I got into my car, got comfortable, lit a joint, and started my way back home.

Chapter 4

When I woke up, I reached over to grab my phone off the nightstand and saw 5 message alerts. I scrolled down the list, still no message from my best friend Michelle. Damn, I thought, this must have really shaken her up more than I would've expected. It had already been about a week since I told her what happened, and I still had not heard anything from her.

An hour later she finally texted me. I was kind of worried if she would not be able to get past what I had told her, but from the looks of it, she seemed to be okay…for now.

"Hey Thomas! Sorry I didn't text you back; I had a lot going on."
"It's cool, I totally understand. I know what I told you was a lot to handle. So, if you have any questions please just ask me and I'll tell you."

"Oh, I know you will tell me, but I'm not worried about that right now. I have to move. I just bought a new house and was going crazy getting together all the paperwork they requested. You will never believe how much shit these people ask for when buying a house. It has me losing my mind. And you can best believe when I say I have a lot to ask you about that night, but I don't know if it's what you think it is."

"Okay, so we're good?" I was still unsure.

"Hell yes we are. So, what are you doing tonight? Do you want to grab a beer or something?"

"I can't, I have plans, but if you are not busy tomorrow, it is a date, kid."

"Sweet, have fun and be safe! I will see you tomorrow. Wait, are you going to meet another female? A new female, I bet, too. Are you retarded? Whatever, I'll see you tomorrow. Please be safe…please."

"Always, kiddo."

I walked over to the kitchen counter, plugged in my phone, and turned the radio up so I could shower and get dressed. I was going to meet this female I met a few weeks back. If the night goes anything close to how our conversations had been going, it was going to be a great night. It should turn into one wild and crazy night, but you never know, so I told myself just to have a good time tonight, with or without her. Once I got into my car, I was just about to let her know I was on my way, but her message came in just before I finish writing.

"Hey, send me a text when you are 5 mins away, so I can unlock the door, and just walk in when you get here," she texts me.

I texted her back, "Ok! But what is your address because I have no clue how to get there?"

She texted the address, "456 Hacksaw Trail, gate code is #1127, 15th floor, apt 1502."

When I was about 5 mins away, I sent her a text that I was close. When I finally arrived, I pulled up to the large cast iron gate that looked like it was hand made. I pulled up to the callbox. I had this crazy obsession about not touching call box number with my fingers, but without realizing I pressed the first digit with my finger. I quickly pulled my finger back and started using my knuckles to put the gate code in. Without any waiting the gate slowly began to open as I made my way up to an empty parking space in the far corner of the lot.

Once I walked upstairs, I knocked once and walked into her apartment. The first thing I noticed before I got completely into the apartment was the hint of a cinnamon apple candle burning. The lights were off, and I could see her on her couch with a single candle burning on the stand.

My eyes instantly zoomed in to watch her fuck herself.

I started walking toward her and dropped to my knees, so I could taste how sweet she really was. As I leaned in she snapped her legs closed.

"What are you doing?" I asked, puzzled.

"Not yet daddy! Do you see that chair over there? Go take a seat and enjoy the show," she said in a sexy soft voice.

With all the excitement I had not seen the single chair in the middle of the living room. As I started walking toward the chair, I could see that there was a set of handcuffs on each arm rest and a pair of leg straps. I slowed down a little.

I could hear her in the background, "Don't you trust me?" I laughed to myself, *bitch I don't know you.*

I sat down in the chair as she started to rub her nipples with an ice cube, once the left nipple was hard she moved on to the next. When she was satisfied that both were as hard as they could be, she reached out and grabbed another piece of ice.

This time she slowly made her way to her belly, lower and lower until she was just above her clit. Her head tilted back with pleasure, and with her other hand, she slipped two fingers inside her wet pussy. I can hear the wetness every time she thrust her fingers inside of herself.

Spreading her pussy, she cried, "I'm about to cum. Oh my God! I'm cumming! Fuck."

When she was done I started to get up. She looked at me.

"No, not yet." She stood up and walked over to cuff me to the chair.

She looked at me with a smile and said, "We're just getting started with you."

At this point my cock was trying to break out of my jeans and she knew it. After all, I was tied up. She walked back into her room. She closed the door behind her, but left it slightly open, I could barely make out her figure walking around her room. Within 5 minutes I could hear her moaning again in pleasure. Once that started, she walked out, stood in front of me, and dropped to her knees. Kissing, rubbing and gently biting the outline of my dick; still in my pants. All I could think about was how hard my dick was. She finally started unzipping my pants and freed my cock and proceed to devour me whole.

The aggressiveness that she demonstrated on my dick was amazing. After about 5 minutes of her choking on my 10 inch stick she looked up at me with smudged mascara and smiled. Then she went back to work on my dick like it was her last meal. I had spit dripping down my nuts. I closed my eyes and tilted my head back to enjoy the bliss of her talent.

All of a sudden I heard a low moan, "Mmm. That black cock looks so good."

I look up and there was a short, beautiful female standing over me. I saw her lick her lips just as she covered my eyes with a blindfold.

I could hear the two ladies giggling and whispering to each other.

"This should be fun." One of the girls said.

No lie, my heart was beating faster and faster by the second. I don't know if it was nerves, the fear of not knowing what was happening, the fact I gave up all control of the situation, or that I had two women ready to fuck me into an early grave, but whatever it was the amount of anticipation was almost overwhelming.

After what felt like a lifetime of waiting, I heard the unknown female whisper in my ear, "Nunca te olvidaremos." (*We will never forget you*).

I had no idea what she said to me, but it made my dick as hard as it could possibly get. She started to lightly nibble on my neck, as her hands made their way down my chest. She started to squeeze and dig her nails into my chest, just as the pain started to take over another feeling came into play.

She had my dick in her hands squeezing the base as she growled. Then there was the sound of her spitting on my dick. I felt her take the tip of my dick and lick and suck on the head, going deeper and deeper down her throat until she began to choke.

"Go deeper! Take all of it." I requested in a deep voice.

Just then the Spanish female behind me, who also had her nails buried into my chest, quickly reached up and grabbed me by the neck; she began to squeeze and pulled me back so she could whisper in my ear.

"You don't give any demands, you don't ask us for anything extra, you will only receive what I feel you deserved at that very moment. Please understand, what I say you can have at one moment does not apply to the next moment. Do you understand what I am saying to you? I need you to tell me if you do."

This bitch is out of her fucking mind, I thought. *Is she thinking I'm going say that shit?* I tried to resist, but the pleasure of what was happening started to take over. In my head I was yelling no; get the fuck away from me, but my body was singing another song.

She whispered again in my ear but with more force, "Do you understand me?"

Surprisingly, I replied, "Yes ma'am I completely understand."

What the fuck did I just say? Not what I meant say. This was so wrong, but it felt so right. The pleasure I was feeling at that moment was more than I had ever encountered.

"Good boy," she said.

"Yes, ma'am whatever you want," I said out of breath.

"Since you have been a good boy, I will reward you by letting you taste me," she said devilishly.

"Okay," I said.

She laughed and said, "Okay! This is how this will work. Let me explain to you and all rules will be followed, and those rules that are broken will have a punishment that will be handed out. Now, when we said something your answer will be 'yes ma'am.' So, let me try this again with you. I will reward you by letting you taste my pussy."

"Yes ma'am. Thank you."

I could hear them moving a table toward me. Then, I could hear her getting on the table.

"Time to eat and do no stop until I'm cumming all over your face," said demanded.

"Yes ma'am," I happily said.

I dove in. Then, I felt another sensation, I was so lost sucking on her sweetness that I didn't realize I was getting my dick sucked on as well. For a minute, I lost track of what I was doing.

"Did I tell you to stop?."

Out of breath I said, "No, you did no..."

I stopped to correct myself. She smacked me so fucking hard my ear started to ring.

Yeah, I'm going to kill this bitch, I thought. Just as I went to break free I felt some type of rod or belt around my neck, and before I knew what was happening, I could not breathe. After a few seconds she loosened it just enough for me to catch some air.

"Now that you see you are not in control of this situation; I will need you to follow any and all directions to the letter Thomas do you understand me clearly. I do not need you to say a word, just nod yes or no, but before you answer, understand that I am in 100% control of how this night will turn out for you. I will ask you again, do you clearly understand me?"

"Yes, ma'am I completely understand all rules and directions must be followed to the letter."

"Good boy! Now, get back to eating and slow it down and enjoy every lick."

This fucking girl was crazy as fuck, and I was still so turned on. I went back to pleasing her the way she wanted. I know I couldn't really do her like I wanted to, but dove in, nonetheless.

I started at the top of her clit making light circular motion with my tongue. After every few circles I traced my tongue down the inside of her pussy lips working my way to the center of her sweet entrance slowly slipping my tongue in and even slower pulling it out savoring the sweet juices of this unknown woman. Then I started making my way back to her clit, but this time applying slightly more pressure. Once I felt her starting to shake I knew what I been working so hard for was coming soon.

I had to stop for a second because I was about close to cumming. *Why?* I realize that her friend was still suck on my cock.

"Fuck I'm about to cum." I moaned.

She stopped and said, "Not yet."

I didn't even have time to bitch before my head was thrust back to my meal, and like a good boy, I went back to eating and sucking on her. The faster I twisted my tongue, the faster she started to shake. Suddenly, I could feel her pussy start to pulsate. I could taste the juices that started to flow from her. I felt like I was eating honey from a jar, and damn it tasted good. Her moans were getting louder and louder until it was a high pitch scream. Her legs started to squeeze my head like a vice grip. Once she was done she stood up and grab me by the face and licked my lips.

She said, "Thomas, you've done great; good boy, now your reward is you finally get to look at me."

I laughed in my head. *My reward is to see her. This bitch thinks she's hotter than what she really is…yeah okay, just take this shit off my eyes.*

At that moment, the blind fold was slowly lifted off my face. The first thing I saw was the leather thigh-high boots. She had thick thighs that instantly had me turned on even more than what I already was. Her hips were wide and her belly was flat.

Shit, this can't be real. I need my glasses, I thought. Her skin complexion was a perfect caramel evenly spread from the top of her head to her feet. She tasted just as good as she looked, and she was much hotter than she thought she was. I could see the white girl was the submissive of the two and was following instruction very well. I could not get the grin off my face. I just kept repeating my head, *this is going to be a great night.* The Spanish woman walked over and untied my legs and she looked at me and smiled.

"Papi, do you smoke?" She asked.

I couldn't take my eyes off her, with a smile on my face I said, "I sure do."

But, I had other ideas on my mind besides smoking. The moment she untied both my arms and legs I leaped up and grabbed her by her hair, and then by her throat. I started to squeeze and walked her back against the wall. I looked over to the other girl and told her to get on her knees. She quickly did what she was told as I turned my attention back to the woman in front of me.

She looked me in the eyes and angrily said, "You better fucking stop."

Before she could finish her sentence, I squeezed even harder, cutting her off; I leaned in closer and whispered in her ear, "You don't give any demands, you don't ask me for anything extra, you will only receive what I feel you deserve at that very moment. Please understand what I say; just because you can have something at that moment it does not apply to the next moment. Do you understand what I am saying to you? All I need you to do is tell me if you understand me."

Her anger began to turn into pleasure and excitement because she knew what I was doing. With my hand still around her neck, I walked her back to the chair. I looked over and the other girl was on her knees waiting for further instruction.

I looked over at her and told her to come tie her friend legs to the chair. She started to stand up and walk toward the chair.

I looked at her and said, "Did I tell you to stand?"

"No sir, you did not," she said as she began to crawl.

Once she was all tied up, I let her go and walked into the kitchen, grabbed another chair, and put it directly in front of the Spanish female. I waited for a few seconds before I said anything to her. I looked at the other female and told her to bring out all of her toys and anything that I could use. She walked into her room and within seconds came back with a big travel bag. I told the white female to get on her knees beside her friend.

"So, ladies ,did y'all have fun playing with me like that? Did y'all enjoy taking control and doing what y'all wanted with me? Well, I hope you did, because the tide has turned and it's my turn to do what I want to do, and this is strictly for my pleasure, but I must admit my pleasure is watching you cum over and over, repeatedly. Just so you know, you will cum more times tonight than you have ever came before in your life, but you will also feel a lot of pain" I said.

I reached into the bag and could feel more restraints that were longer and thicker. I smiled because of the ideas that came to me. I stood up and walked over to the dining room table and pulled it closer to where she was sitting. I pulled out all the toys she had in her bag and I looked at them.

"This I going to be a lot of fun."

The first thing I grabbed was the silver nipple clamps. As I started getting the clamps out, I quickly realized this had a chain that connected the nipple clamps and it also had a vibrating clamp for the clit. I unwrapped the clit clamp and place it on her clit and turn it on to the lowest level. You could see that she was enjoying it. I then pulled a bar that was about three feet long and it had straps on both ends. I bent down and attached the straps to each ankle. I looked at both of them and smiled.

Chapter 5

The day was young, and I wanted to go the gym, but I knew I would run into Mindy. I was supposed to meet her at the bar last night; I was hoping she didn't make it out last night because it would have been a shame to miss the chance to hang out with her.

I made a cup of coffee, no cream or sugar, and walked out to my back porch to kick my feet up. As I was sitting there, that crazy unexpected night started going through my head, but with so many more details this time. Dammit, that night was crazier than I had originally remembered. I smiled as I mentally replayed that night...

I pulled up to this gorgeous, well-lit, free-standing 3-story building. The parking lot was half filled with some of the most beautiful cars and trucks. I pulled my all-black Dodge Charger Hellcat up to the valet parking. Once the attendee walked to my driver side, I opened the door and got out. I could see the youthful smile and him nodding his head high in approval.

"Sir, please excuse my French, but that's a bad ass car," he said.

I always love when people lust over my girl. I looked at him smiled and said, "Yes, thank you, she's a good girl. You can take it around the block for a spin, just be careful."

He looked at me, laughed, and said, "Yeah right...I wish. I can't even afford to put a full tank of gas in there."

As the valet hopped into the car, I replied, "Okay young man, it's your call, but if you change your mind just be careful please."

"Sir, that would be a dream to drive your car, because it is my dream car, but it's against company policy for me to do that. Besides, if something did happen, the company would be held liable for that. I don't get paid much, but I do like what I do. I have to say thanks, but no thanks, and thank you for offering."

"Okay, no worries, but when I leave make sure you give me your number, or I'll give you my number and we can take it from there. So, if you want to, we can take it for a spin…off the clock." I said to the kid.

I started walking toward the building with no intention of him ever driving my car outside of taking it to the parking lot. When I heard my car engine come to life. I stopped and turned to look back and the kid had the biggest smile on his face. He looked at me and gave me a thumbs up. I smiled back and gave him a nod in approval. I turned and headed back to the building.
Once I entered the building, I stopped and scanned the large open area for the restroom, but to my dismay I did not find one. I saw this really beautiful black woman standing behind a large, all-mirrored counter. We made eye contact and she smiled. I smiled back and made my way to her desk. About half-way to her there, I was cut off by my ex-girlfriend and a group of her friends.

We had ended things on bad terms. Long story short, she said that I was overweight and that she felt that I wasn't emotionally ready for a woman like her. As soon as we broke up I made changes in my life lost 60lbs and upgraded my image.

"Oh my God, Thomas is that you? WOW! You look great," she said.

Knowing exactly who she was, I extended my hand to shake her hand and said, "Yes I'm Thomas, and you are?"

She perked her head up in shocked with her voice cracking and said, "Wow... Really? Why are you acting like you don't know exactly who I am? You were never good at lying."

I stood there and stared at her, hoping I could keep this up without laughing in her face. I was thinking how beautiful she still was after all these years. Body still on point, outfit perfectly put together, and not on damn hair out of place. I thought to myself, *fuck, I was hoping that bitch would have fallen off the next time I saw her, but nope, I can't get that lucky.*

"Thomas, are you serious? You really don't remember me? Ouch, but I do deserve that I guess. Anyway, it's me, Dana," she said.

I just stared at her without saying a word. She stared back at me waiting to get a response. This went on for what felt like forever. I saw her eyes slowly scan me from head to toe, noticing all the changes and hard work I had put into improving myself. Once I felt she had taken in all that I thought she need to, I widened my eyes as if a light was turned on.

"Oh, Dana. Okay, now I remember. How have you been? It's been a long time," I said.

"Yeah! What two, three years, right?"

"Yes, I believe so."

"You look great. I see life has been good to you."

"Yeah, it been good. I can't complain too much, and if I did no one would care anyway."

"No, that's not true, I always cared."

I laughed, "Well, anyways what's new with you? Married yet?"

"I been good. Working a lot as always and going to the gym, but I see you been hitting the gym pretty hard, too. I'm not married yet, but I am seeing someone. Anyways, you look amazing."

"Thank you."

"No! You really look great, and I see you are hitting the gym really hard too."

"I have been. Trying to get my sexy back, that's all."

"You always been sexy."

"Really? I could have sworn I was overweight at some point, but maybe that was me in my own head."

She lowered her eyes and said, "Yeah! Sometimes you do that. So, where are you living now? Same place or didn't you move?"

"No, I moved about a year ago. I bought about 15 acres and built a house on it. Nothing too big or fancy, just something I can relax in."

"Wow! Did you get a new job?"

"I started my own company about two years ago and I also remodel homes."

"Do you rent them or sell?"

"Both!"

"Very nice; I always knew you could do it."

I laughed again and said, "Yeah, you always believed in me."

"I see you took my advice on changing how you dressed."

"If you say so."

I looked over her shoulder and could see her friends looking over at me smiling, so I returned the smile. One of her friend's eyes lit up and she screamed, "Holy fuck! Thomas is that you? Is that my brother from another mother?"

Dana turned around and said, "Yes! Yes, girl, that's Thomas."

She ran over and jumped in my arms and gave me a big hug. Elizabeth was the only friend of Dana's I liked. The rest of them were total gold diggers and only cared for what a man could buy them. As she was hugging me, I heard her say how much she missed me. She even said sorry about how Dana and I had broken up.

Once I let go of her, the rest of her friends walked over and I didn't recognize any of them; it looked like she had a whole new group of friends.

One of the girls said, "Well, are you guys going to introduce us to this fine chocolate man or are you two planning on keeping him yourselves?"

Elizabeth turned and said, "Y'all won't believe it, but this is Dana's ex Thomas, and my brother from another mother."

The girls smiled and I went to shake their hands. "Very nice to meet you ladies. I hope you beautiful ladies have a great and safe night." I then looked over at Dana and Elizabeth.

"Baby-girl it was great seeing you ladies; I have to get inside and find a seat."

"We have a booth if would you like to sit with us."

"Thanks, but no thanks. I have a table!"

Dana looked at me and said, "Are you meeting someone here? I don't want to keep your date waiting."

"Naw y'all good - I'm here alone."

One of her friends said in a low voice, "Damn, girl you hear that? He's here alone. What a waste of some good dick."

Dana said, "So why not come hang out with us?"

"Well, because I came here to just chill and have a relaxing chill night. Nothing personal."

She turned and started walking away and said "Whatever, your loss."

I laughed out loud and said, "I see you are still a bitch! Guess some things never change."

"Fuck you Thomas," said spat.

"You wish," I said.

"Been there, done that," she returned.

I could only laugh at that point. Elizabeth walked up to me, hugged me, and gave me her number; she said to give her a call. I nodded my head and said okay.

As the group was walking away, one of their friends smiled and said to me, "You can call me anytime…day or night." She grabbed my hand and passed me a folded piece of paper.

Once they were out of sight I looked down and she had left her name and number and a message that said to call her. I just shook my head and put the paper in my pocket.

When I was finally able to reach the front desk girl, she was still standing in the same place with the same big smile on her face.

"Hello Sir, how are you doing today? I'm April! How can I help you?"

"Well! Hello April, you have a beautiful bright smile, I'm Thomas."

"Pleased to meet you, sir. What can I do for you?"

"The bathroom! Where can I find the bathroom?"

"Okay! If you walk down to the end of the hallway, make your first right. Then you will past an elevator on the left, go just past those doors and you will see the restrooms."

"Thank you and you have a good night. Don't work too hard."

After the front desk girl pointed me in the right direction, I turned the corner and made may way toward the bathroom. I saw a quick glance of what seemed to be an angel in a red dress.

I walked into the bathroom and went to the mirror to make a few last second adjustments to my perfectly fitted black suit. I looked in the mirror and smiled at myself.

Damn boy, you look right.

I turned and the bathroom attendant asked me if I would like some cologne. I looked to see if he had what I was wearing, and to my surprise, he did; he had a small bottle of *Cool Water*. He reached over and sprayed some on a paper tab and gave it to me. I thanked him and dropped two bucks in his tip jar.

I walked out of the bathroom and made my way to the jazz lounge. I stood at the entry way and found a server to help me to my table. As we walked to toward my table, I instantly spotted the most beautiful woman I have ever laid eyes on, and we locked eyes. I smiled at her and made my way over to the small table toward the back of the room. Every few steps I would glance over in her direction to see if she was still looking; to my delight, she was.

I sat down and tried to redirect my attention to the band on stage, but that was short lived. I could not keep my eyes off of her. I saw that her eyes were filled with just as much lust as I had in my own.

She stood up from her table and headed towards the back exit, but I was in her direct path. She was no taller than 5'5" with her heels on. She had thick, curly jet-black hair with a slight angel's breath of light brown highlights, perfectly placed by God himself. Her eyes were light brown and could penetrate the soul of the most hardened person. She wore a tight, beautiful blood red dress that came down about six inches above her knee, but you could only see a small portion of her perfect brown skin, because of the sexiest thigh-high, high-heeled boots. With every step she took toward me, my body temperature went up one degree. There was no one else in this building that I wanted. As she walked to me, our eyes locked and neither of us looked away. My palms started to sweat; my mouth suddenly became dry. She was about 10 feet away from me and I decided that I was going to speak to her. This might be my only chance. Now she was 5 feet away, and it felt as though it was only her and I in this whole place.

"Excuse me sir; sir, excuse me. Can I get you something to drink?" a waiter asked.

In that moment, I was brought back to reality, and she swiftly and gracefully walked past me towards the bathroom. At first, I looked at the waiter like he did something wrong, but then started to smile to myself.

"Yes, sir can I please have a double of crown apple and a splash of Sprite please, and a glass of water," I said.

When the waiter returned, he asked if I wanted to order food at that time, but I passed on the food for now.
As he was walking away, I saw her returning from the bathroom, heading right towards me. She placed her hand

lightly on my shoulder; I reached up to touch her perfect skin, just as I did, she slipped me a note.

Meet me at...

Chapter 6

When I finally came back to reality after being taken away by the revised version of my memory, I stood up and made my way back to my room to start getting dressed for the gym. When I was ready to go, I grabbed a joint out of my desk and took it with me so I could have it after my workout. I walked into the gym and the first person I saw was Mindy, but she did not have her usual happy face. She made a beeline to me like a pissed off woman, and everyone knows not to play with a pissed off woman. I just stood there bracing myself for the storm. It definitely came, but to my surprise it wasn't aimed toward me. And I was grateful for that.

After about 5 minutes of her venting to me she looked at me and said, "Oh, Thomas, I'm so sorry I have to say sorry twice.

I look at her confused a little and said, "Okay?"

"One, for talking your head off right now about my husband, and two, because I never showed up last night. I felt so bad. I took a shower and sat on the couch, got comfortable, and the next thing I knew I was waking up this morning," she said in a low sweet voice.

"No, it's no problem. I totally understand. I didn't stay too long, and honestly I wasn't expecting you to come," I said in response.

"I'm sorry, I promise I'll come tonight if you go. It was good talking to you, but I have to go back to work. Oh, before you leave, give me your number. I want to make sure you are going to go if I do decide to come," she said.

"I can do that," I said as I walked toward the stationary bike to get my 5-mile warm up. About halfway through my workout I received a text from Marquita. I looked down at the message and she was asking if she could see me again. I thought to myself how much fun I had with her and I would love to see how far I could press my limits with her. I texted her back and told her that I was busy the next two days, but that on Monday night, I would love to meet up with her.

"Hey, Thomas, I have to ask you a question. Please don't take this the wrong way," Marquita texted.

"What's up sweetheart? Ask away," I texted in response.

"Do you remember when we were talking at the bar about the one fantasy that I have all ways wanted? The one I said that was unexpectedly hard to get with black men," she texted.

I replied back, "Baby girl, do you know how much shit we talked about? We talked about all type of crazy shit that night. You have to narrow this down a lot for me."

"When I was talking about having two black men at once."

"Oh! Yea, I remember now."

"So, do you know another guy that would be down with something like that? I know. I'm not saying it has to be soon, but I wanted to put that bug into your ear in case you know someone that would be down with that."

"I might know someone, but he's out of town for the next few weeks. I'll hit him up when he gets back into town."

"Thank you, Sir."

I put the phone down and went back to my work out. When I was done working out, I walked into the bathroom, grabbed my bags to head home. Once I got to my car, I saw another note on my window. This time when I read it, I pulled my phone out and started to text the number on the note. I knew it was the same girl from the other day, so I didn't want to forget this time.

By the time I got home she had already texted me back, and her reply had me laughing out loud.

"It's about time you hit me up." she texted back.

"Sorry! I'm a busy man. How are you?"

"I'm good, just getting out the shower," she said.

"Very nice. So you nice and wet."

She texted back with one word, all capital letters, "LAME!

I laughed and typed, "I never claimed to be the smoothest talker in the world."

"Yep, and I see why. LOL. I saw you a few days ago in the parking lot and wanted to reach out to you to see if we could get to know each other."

"Well that sounds good to me, but I do have one request if you don't mind, "I said.

"Sure! What's the request?"

I replied, "Well, I would love to at least know who I'm talking to. Would you be okay sending me a picture?"

"Okay, but first let me ask you a question. How would you feel if you were to get to know me without knowing what I look like? What if I only tell you what I look like and not show you? I want you to know me. Get to know me for who I am as a person. Would you be okay with something like that?"

I was just talking to my homegirl about this. So, I texted her back, "Sure! I think I can do that. Not going to lie, I have never done anything like this before, but I'm willing to try it. The only thing is you have to tell me what you look like."

"I can't really tell you what I look like because I'm not the normal type of female that most guys like. I can tell you that I am 4'10", 135lbs and mixed race, that's all I can give you, but I can also promise that you will not be disappointed," she said to me.

"I'll take your word for it. Can I text you later? I'm about to take a shower and go out for dinner and drinks."

"Okay. I look forward to getting to know you, Mr. Thomas," she said.
"Looking forward to it, too, my mystery girl," I said.

I set my phone alarm for 7pm that night. I then walked into the living room, turned on my surround sound, and put on a good movie. I knew I had at least 2 hours before I had to get dressed. I lit a joint and laid down to relax for a little before I had to get going. I was playing on my phone when I got another text from Marquita.

"WYD?" she asked.

"Chilling, watching T.V. about to take a nap," I said to her.

"I have a friend that wants to meet you. She has never had any black cock. She would love to get fucked hard, but her problem is that her husband isn't that big. I was telling her how big your cock was and she asked if she can meet you. I'm not saying you will fuck her or have to fuck her, but I think you two would get along well. So, would this be something you would be down with?"

"Yeah! I'd be down for that. I think it would be fun. Have you and her ever played together before?"

"No! We worked together for a few years, and we just clicked."

"Okay! That's cool. I'm about to take a quick power nap. I'll text you later," I said.

I propped my feet up on my black leather couch and within minutes I was in a deep sleep. I started dreaming of the night again, but the craziest part of it all was that it was so real.

I looked down at the note and it read, *Meet me in the parking lot of the Classic Garden. I will be in a white BMW trimmed in black.*

I sat there smiling and thinking how lucky I was. With the biggest smile on my face I looked up. When I looked up, I locked eyes with my ex. If looks could kill I would've been dead, she was sitting there with venom in her eyes and hatred in her heart. I stared back at her and returned her anger with an ear to ear smile showing my newly cleaned white teeth.

She stood up and walked over to me and sat down at my table and said, "Who the fuck is that?"

"Who is who? I don't know who the fuck you are talking about."

"Don't play me Thomas."

"Okay! Let get this straight, right now. You and I are not together. You gave up that right to ask me any fucking thing the day you walked out on me. I have not fucked with you. I have not called you; I have not talked to any of your friends. I have given you nothing but the space that you wanted and needed. Now, you want to come fuck with me and cause a scene in front of people? You made your choice, and I was not included in that plan. Wait a second, didn't you say you were getting married soon?"

"Yes! I am, but I'm still in love with you. I think of you all the time. I know I was wrong. I know I didn't give you the chance to fix the relationship, but I have grown over the years. I am a better person."

"No, Dana. I'm done. To be honest with you, I don't even want to be friends with you. I will always love you but you are not a good person. You can put on that show for other people, but I will not fall for that shit. I know you. It took me a long time to come to terms that you are just a bad person, so please stop."

I sat there and stared into her eyes without a touch of remorse for what I had just told her. She needed to know. I needed to tell her. I didn't hate her at all, but I also didn't like her. The craziest part was that at one point in my life, I loved her more than life itself. Now, there was nothing. She looked at me with confusion and hurt in her eyes.

"Thomas! I was good to you. I loved you."

"Dana, stop! I'm not going to do this with you. There's no need for you to sit here and explain anything to me. There's no reason for me to explain to you why I said what I said."

"Are you fucking kidding me right now? Fuck you, Thomas! You are just going to sit there like your shit doesn't stink, like because you lost a few pounds and made a little money, now you all that. Nope, you still ain't shit motherfucker."

"It's cool baby girl, I know. And I'm sorry you feel that way. Good luck with whatever you are looking for Bitch." I responded with a stone-cold expression on my face.

She looked me in my face and spit directly on me, stood up yelled, "Fuck you!" She then threw a glass of water in my face. All I could do was shake my head. She was still the same person. I wasn't going to let that bitch fuck up my night. I reached over and grabbed the napkin and cleaned my face off and dried my shirt the best that I could.

After about five minutes of hearing people whisper, I stood up and walked to the bathroom to finishing straightening myself up. Once I was in the bathroom, a guy walked in not 30 seconds after me and said, "Man you are a better man than me. I would have fucked that bitch up."

I just laughed, "Yeah, man it's hard. Lord knows I wanted to fuck her up, but I can't, too much to lose. Well, that and my mom would fuck me up, too."

He shook his head, "Yeah! That's true; mom dukes don't play those games."

"Okay pimping, be good."

"You too, homie."

I walked out of the bathroom and made my way back to the table to watch the rest of the show. As I sat there, a few people walked up to me and mentioned to me that they had heard what was said and saw what had happened and wanted to say that I handled it like a gentleman. I thanked them and kept watching the show.

About 30 minutes had passed since I received the note, so I felt enough time had passed. I signaled for the server to bring the tab. Once he got to the table, I asked him if I gave him my valet ticket if he could have my car ready. Before leaving I asked the server to deliver two bottles of champagne to Dana's table. I paid the tab and left a sizable a tip for the extra service that he extended to me. I stood and smiled at the table where my ex sat, and then turned and walked away.

Once I got to close to the front glass door, I could hear my car pulling up to the front of the building. I made my way down the stairs to the curb and saw the kid get out the car and he had the same smile on his face when I first saw him earlier driving off in my car.

I walked over to the car and walked to the driver side and smiled and said, "You didn't fuck it up, did you?"

His eye widened and he said, "Hell no! I hit the gas a few times.

I smiled and said, "Okay, it's all good. Thanks for taking such great care of her."

I reached in my pocket and grabbed 50 bucks and gave it to him, telling him to have a goodnight. I turned toward the building, and saw my ex standing in the door staring at me, so I waved at her before I got into my car.

I sat in my car and got myself comfortable with my music coming out of my two 12-inch custom sound system. I hit the gas to really bring the engine alive. I pulled off and slowly made my way to the road. Once I was on the road, I dropped the gear down, hit the gas, and the engine roared to life. Everyone in the parking lot turned to look at me pulling off. About two miles down the road, I merged onto the highway. Once on the highway, I put in the GPS the address the lady gave me. The place was supposed to be 30 minutes away, but like everyone else, I figured I could get there in 20 mins. About 19 mins later I pulled up to this nearly empty parking lot.

I saw the BMW, pulled up to it, and rolled down the widow. The woman looked at me with a big smile on her face. She was as beautiful as I thought she was going to be. I stared at her.

She said, "Follow me! And you better fuck me like I want to be fucked."

I looked at her in shock and said, "Excuse me. What did you say to me?"

She repeated, "You heard what the fuck I said. I need you to fuck me. I don't need you to make love to me; I have a husband at home to do that. I need you to be treat like a dirty whore. If you can't do that tell me now and we can go our separate ways no hard feelings."

I looked at her and said, "That's what I thought you said. Do you have a place to go or would you like to follow me?"

"No follow me! Actually, get in I'll drive."

"I don't know you like that. You might try to kidnap me and kill me."

"Yep my little ass might kidnap you. Just get in the fucking car. But you know me enough to fuck me."

"Okay, you have a point."

I got out of my car, took almost everything out of my pocket, and left it in the center console after I grabbed a gold wrapper. I got out of the car and locked the doors. I walked around to her passenger door and got inside her car. She drove about 3 more miles down the road and turned down to this abounded warehouse district and pulled behind a warehouse that had about 30 loading docks.

She parked beside a green empty dumpster. We both got out of the car and she started walking around the front of the car toward me. She started to kiss me, and I grabbed her by the neck and just shook my head.

I looked at her and said, "Oh no, you have a husband at home for that shit. Get on your knees."

She looked at me with pure lust and said, "Yes sir."

She squatted down and took my dick into her mouth and started sucking my dick as if she hadn't sucked on a dick in years. I leaned my head back to enjoy her talent. I looked down at her and realized she wasn't doing what I said. I pulled my dick out of her mouth and reached down and grabbed her by her hair and pulled her up to face me.

"I thought I said to get on your knees. I did not say squat; I said your knees. You wanted to be treated like a dirty whore. Well, I'm going to treat you as such. Do you understand me?"

"Yes Sir! I do understand, I will do better I promise."

"Good! Then get on your knees and do as you are told you fucking whore."

After a few more minutes of her sucking on my dick, she pulled my dick out and started begging me to fuck her. I told her to stand up and turn around. Like a good girl she did what she was told. I pull on the condom and slipped inside of her from behind. She was so wet.

She yelled, "Oh my God please fuck me like the whore I am."

I started fucking her harder and faster. I grabbed her by the hair and pulled her head back. I started getting more and more turned on the harder and rougher I got with her. I flipped her over and pulled on her back and lifted her legs up and started fucked her again, but I wasn't able to get as deep as I wanted because of the angle of the front hood of the car.

We walked to the back of her car and she sat on the trunk and I slipped inside her perfectly. Yes, this was what I needed. This is what she needed. I was balls deep.

I reached up and started choking her and she started to smile. I could feel her cumming all over me, I could feel her cum dripping. It was so good that I lost myself in what was going on. I kept fucking her harder, faster, deeper, until I started to cum.

I didn't realize that she was tapping on my forearm for the last few minutes. When I did realize what was going on, her body was limp and lifeless.

I jumped back, shocked, trying to catch my breath, but I wasn't able to. I just stood there with my pants down around me knees. What had I done?

Her lifeless body slide down the back of the car onto the ground. Her eyes were still open, her face and make-up were still flawless. I just stood there in disbelief. When I finally came back to reality, I knew I had to get out of there. I pulled my pants up and turned and started to run, but halfway down the parking lot I stop and turned around. I had to go back and wipe that car down. I had to make sure my fingerprints were not on or in that car, or anything else I had touched.

Once I finished trying to clean things up the best I could, I ran the three or four miles back to my car, making sure to stay off the main road and keeping out of sight of the oncoming cars. An hour later I was finally safe in my car. Sweat was dripping down my face. I reached up to the overhead visor and grabbed a joint out before starting my car up. Just as I started my car, I saw a police car racing in the direction I just came from. How did they find her so fast?

I waited a few more minutes before I started my car. Once I felt it was safe, I lit the joint, took a hit, and started my car. I didn't know where I was exactly, so I had to put my address in my GPS and saw my house was an hour away. I thought to myself this might be the longest drive of my life.

The directions to get to the highway took me back the same way as her body. I paused and collected myself for a moment. A mile down the road I saw flashing lights quickly coming up behind me. I started to speed up. I was now going 10 miles over the speed limit. All I could think was, *How did they find me so fast? They couldn't have. Could they? Slow down!*

The lights got closer and closer. My heart started to beat faster and faster. *This can't be happening. It was a mistake. I didn't try or want to do it. It was an accident.*

I decided to slow down and take my chances in court. I was about a mile ahead of the warehouse district and about 1,000 feet from the highway. I was about to pull over to the shoulder when the police shot pass me going about 100mph.

I could finally exhale.

Once I pulled over to the shoulder of the road, I leaned forward and rested my head on the steering wheel. My body started to relax. Every muscle was sore. I sat there for about 5 minutes. I suddenly looked down and noticed my hands were still tightly gripping the steering wheel, to the point that my knuckles were turning purple from the lack of blood flow. I slowly started loosening my grip and started to feel the blood rushing back into my hands. Once I could finally release my grip completely, I sat back and started collecting my thoughts about what happened, and what almost just happened. I sat there for another 10 minutes before I slowly pulled back onto the highway to head home. I finally saw my exit coming into view and put my signal on to exit the highway; when I did, I looked down at my wrist and realized that I had left my new watch in her console.

I could not take the chance of going back to get it. I was just praying that there was nothing to link me to her. I shook my head and said a quick prayer. I saw the lights to my driveway and decided to drive past it and take the side road to my property.

At that moment my alarm started to ring waking me up from my much-needed nap.

Chapter 7

As I was on the couch playing on my phone, my best friend Michelle walked in with a smile on her face. It wasn't a happy smile, but a devilish grin. I sat up on my couch and shook my head. I just knew this would be the conversation I have been avoiding and not wanting to have. She walked over to the bar and grabbed a bottle of Tito's and made herself a drink.

She looked at me and said, "Hey! Are you ready to talk to me? I have a few questions for you."

I looked at her confused and slowly said, "Questions? What type of question do you have?

"Really Thomas, don't play stupid."

I laughed and said, "Okay, let's get this over."

"So, let me get this straight, because I want to make sure I understand what's going on. When you first told me, it kind of took me off guard. Okay, so how did you do it?"

"I choked her."

"With what?"
"My hand!"

"Wait, you used your bare hands? She must have really pissed you off."

"Well, it wasn't even like that. It was during sex on the trunk of her car. I met her at the jazz club. She passed me a note for me to meet her somewhere. It was so fucking hot. No words exchanged between us. It was instant attraction."

"Did anyone see ya'll together?"

"No! I met her in an empty parking lot. Then, I got into her car and we drove to an abandon warehouse district."

"You got into her car. Please tell me you clean the car and didn't leave anything in there."

"Well, kind of."

"What the fuck does 'kinda' mean? You clean it or you didn't."

"Well, you remember that new watch I just got?"

"You mean the new watch that I got for you? The same watch that you registered so that if it got stolen you would find it if it was pawned? You mean that watch."

"Yes, that watch, but I never registered it so there's nothing linking me to it."

"Oh, okay! Man, you are fucking crazy. So how did it feel?"

"Actually, I don't know, because we were fucking, and I started to choke her and I guess I choked her to long and too hard. It was a mistake. I feel really bad, I think."

"What you mean you think you feel bad?"

"Well I felt bad because I thought I was going to get caught, but right now I have no regrets. I know that isn't right. I'm just waiting for it to hit me and send me into a depression. It's crazy because I'm getting more turned-on during sex when I think about it."

"I have to be honest; I have always wanted to do that. That's my biggest fantasy. I want to feel the power of having someone's life in my hands. I have already planned it out down to the details of where and how to hide the body."

"What girl, are you crazy? This wasn't planned. This is all wrong on so many levels. We shouldn't be talking about this."

"Yeah, we shouldn't be doing a lot of things, but here we are doing this. Do you want to do it again?"

"I have replayed that night in my head over and over again and I do not have the desire to do that again, EVER!"

"Well, if it does happen again and you need anything, know I'm here for you; no need to hide it."

"Okay kiddo, I hear you."

We sat and had a few drinks and talked more. I went into more details of that night. I must be honest I wasn't expecting this response from her. She was more into this than I have seen her in a long time. About five drinks later, she stood up and started to get ready to leave. I asked if she was okay to drive.

She looked at me, laughed, and said, "I'm not a lightweight like you. I'll call you tomorrow and stay out of trouble. Love you kid." Then she turned and walked out the front door.

I walked into the kitchen and made me a sandwich before heading back into the living room and started rolling a blunt before I had to head out to the bar.

Chapter 8

I pulled up to the bar and parked in the back corner of the parking lot. It wasn't very packed inside, but the crowd was large enough to make you want to hang out and people watch. I walked in and was greeted by my favorite bartender.

She was a bigger female, but I thought she was beautiful and oozed sex appeal. She had a very bright and happy personality, and her hair always showed her brightness. Today her hot pink hair was pulled back in a ponytail, shining from sweat. She was about 5'8" and had to be about 180lbs but had curves that most ladies would kill for. She had it all in the chest, ass, and those perfect thighs. She was white mixed with Hawaiian with thick, full lips and her eyes screamed *fuck me*. She was never flirty, but the way she looked at you made you feel as though she wanted it.

I always thought she was beautiful, but I also knew she was good at her work, and her job was not only to give you drinks, but to work it so you gave her a nice tip when you leave. I smiled at her and she walked over and put a beer in front of me.

"Hey, handsome how are you," the bartender said.

"I'm good, baby girl. I love your hair. Hot pink, yes, yes it's so you, I fucking love it," I said to her.

"Really?! Thanks, I was kinda worried about having two in it," she said.

"What, two colors? I know I wear glasses, but I only see pink" "Oh, that's right, you haven't seen it down. Yeah, there's actually purple when I let it down," she said.

"Well, are you going to let it down so I can see it?"

"Really?"

"Yes," I said.

"Wait until it calms down a little and I will. Promise."

"Okay, I'll be here."

I looked up and saw Mindy walking in the door and it completely caught me off guard. I was hoping she would come but figured she wouldn't since she was married and happy at home. When she walked in, she stopped about 5 feet inside and looked around. We locked eyes and she got the biggest smile on her face. I returned the smile and motioned for her to come sit down with me. As she started walking toward me, I got a good look at her body and it was so much nicer than I realized. She was about 5'3" and built like a softball catcher. Her legs were nice and thick as they curved with the grace of an artist.

When she got next to me, I stood up and pulled the chair out for her to sit down.

"Thank you! What...no hug? I want one of those big bear-hugs I know you give out."

I looked at her, smiled, "Girl, whatever you want."

I took a step forward and hugged her. I could feel her exhale and sink closer to me.

"Thank you! You don't know how much I need this hug right now."

When she finally pulled away, I ask her what she wanted to drink.

"I will have a White Claw," she said.

I looked at her and laughed, "A white what?"

"It's a white girl drink," she said.

The bartender looked at me and laughed, "Hell, I know a lot of guys that drink those. You should at least try it. You might actually like it."

I stood up from the bar, and they both looked at me and I know they wanted to know what I was doing. I grabbed my balls.

"Yep, I got nuts. Sorry, I still have my balls, so I'll pass on that shit."
Mindy looked at me and laughed. "You're drinking Bud Light, same fucking things, asshole!"

"Y'all got jokes I see. It's cool, I can take it, but I hope y'all can take it when I dish it out, too."

Mindy looked at me and with a devilish grin and said, "I can take a lot more than you think."

The bartender looked at me and smiled and said, "Thomas you might have your hands full with this one right here."

I smiled at her as she turned and walked away. I turned my attention back to Mindy and all her sexiness.

"Glad you came out. I have to be honest I wasn't expecting you to come."

"To be honest, Thomas, I wasn't going to come. I talked to my husband and he was the one that convinced me to actually come out," she said.

I looked at her with a puzzled look on my face, "I'm sorry, what did you just say?"

She smiled and said, "Yes, my husband told me to come. I'm a little nervous to be here because I have never done this before."

"I'm a little confused right now. First, does your husband know you are out with another man? Second…never done what? We are just having a few drinks nothing more, so there's no need to be nervous," I said to her.

"Thomas I will not lie to you. I think you are extremely attractive and to be honest more of the girls at the gym think the same. They always ask me about you because you've only talked to me. Yes, you speak to everyone, but you have not had a conversation with anyone else besides me. You are a mystery to them," she replied, matter-of-factly.

"Oh, shit! Really? Are you just trying to make me feel special?"

"No, not at all."

We sat there and talked about so much. I learned that she was a retired Army Veteran and was wounded in duty. Her and her husband had been together since middle school and they had never broken up for any amount of time. She had two boys, 14 and 10 years old. She was a little sister of three girls. The most impressive of everything I learned about her was that she was finishing up her master's in behavior modification. We even talked about my past and about my time in prison, my abusive stepdad, my kids, and my life goals.

It was a refreshing night to actually talk to someone. I had never opened up to anyone like this before. It made me more attracted to her, but she was that forbidden fruit not to be touched.
All of a sudden the music stopped, and the light came on in the bar, and I realized that we were the only people in the bar. The bartenders were mopping the floors and all the chairs had been flipped upside down and put on the tables. The bartender walked up to me and said, "Do y'all plan on going home anytime soon, because we do."

We laughed, thanked the staff, stood up and started walking towards the door. I looked at Mindy and asked her where she was parked so I could walk her to her car. She pointed toward the same area where I was parked.

I looked at her and said, "You parked right next to me. Nice, is that your truck?"

"Yes that's my little baby. That's your black dodge?"

"Yep that's my girl," I said.

She smiled and asked me if I wanted to come over for a night cap. Every bit of common sense told me to respectfully pass on it. In my head I said no, but the words that came out my mouth were the complete opposite of what I meant. Once again, my dick spoke for me. Dammit, why do I always get myself into shit I shouldn't be in?

When we pulled up to her house it was absolutely beautiful. We walked in and I followed her into the kitchen towards her oversized kitchen island. She made me a drink and we continued with the conversion that we started at the bar. Maybe an hour went by and she said, "I'll be right back. I have to put on something more comfortable."

She walked into her bedroom and walked right back out with a large bag of weed and asked if I smoke. She put the bag of weed on the counter.

"There's papers over there; roll up and I'll be right back."

She was gone for ten minutes and when she walked back out, she was barefoot, wearing a thin bathrobe with her hair flowing down to her mid-back.

"Now I feel so much better." She stopped in front of me and then walked over to make me another drink. I stood up and walked to the end of the kitchen island to grab the lighter to fire it up. I smiled at her and lit the joint.

When I turned back around to face her, she dropped her robe and my eyes widened. The joint dropped out of my mouth and hit the ground. She walked toward me and said, "I have wanted this since I first saw you."

Chapter 9

The light started creeping in through my window. I walked over and pressed the button to let down the storm shutters, causing my room to go totally dark. I set my alarm for 9:00am and went back to bed.

When my alarm started to go off, I popped right out of bed and walked to the living room and turned on my music. Before I got to the shower, I texted a friend and asked if he was busy tonight because I had something, I wanted to do with him. I said that I would text him with the details of what I had planned in a few hours. I set my schedule for the day, including meeting up with my accountant, making sure the renovations were going as planned, and that the completion dates were still on schedule. It was about 6:00pm when I got a text back from my friend Chris asking about tonight.

I texted back, "What's good homie, how have you been? Sorry man I got crazy busy with working and running around trying to make sure I hit these dates for these houses I just bought."

"It's cool ,brother! So what's the deal with tonight? What do you have planned?"

"Okay, so I have this chick that I linked up with a few weeks ago. Well, I actually met her about a year ago, but we never hooked up and pretty much just lost contact with each other. But we ended up hooking up a few weeks ago and wow…she's a wild one. So, I wanted to know if you are down?"

"Hell yea, I'm down with you brother," he said.

I replied back to him, "Okay, cool, so the thing is you can fuck her as hard as you want, and all holes are open. Her safe word is Red. Her only two rules are no phones in the room; they have to be left on the kitchen table, and always wear condoms. Other than that, its free game."

"Okay! What time are you thinking?"

I texted, "I'm going to send you a meetup location, then you can ride with me into her complex. How does 8pm work for you?"

He replied, "8pm is perfect. See you there pimpin."

I pulled my phone out and texted Shannon to see what she had planned for the evening. I planned to make her fantasy come true tonight.

"Hello Sir! How are you? How can I serve you today?" she texted.

"I'm going to give you some instructions. I'm going to come by tonight around 8ish. I want you with your collar on."

She replied, "Yes sir, as you desire."

"I also need you to have a blind fold on. I will send you more directions later. Okay?"

"Yes Sir."

I walked to the bathroom and started to shave myself from head to toe, I trimmed my beard down to a sharp, clean-edged look. I grabbed my phone, put on some music, and walked back into the bathroom to finished getting dressed for the night. I grabbed the keys off the hook that was hanging by the door. Tonight, I was feeling myself a little more than normal. Instead of driving my Challenger, which always turned heads, I was in the mood to go big. So, I switched and grabbed my truck keys. My truck was beautiful, and I usually only brought her out on the weekends for a show or a special event. I climbed in and pushed the button to bring her to life, her roar always made me smile.

I pulled up to the location right at 8:00pm on the dot and Chris was already there waiting on me. Before I talked to Chris I texted Shannon and told her that along with the blindfold, I also wanted her to have her ear buds in and have the music playing so she couldn't hear anything. Without any questions she agreed.

I rolled my window down, looked at Chris, and said, "What's up homie?"

"Chilling brother. How are you? So, what's the deal with this chick," he said.

"Okay! She does not know that I'm bringing you with me, but this has always been one of her fantasies and with tonight being Christmas I figured, why not? Feel me? So right now, she has on her blindfold and her earbuds in, so she will not know when we walk in and she will not know you are there. Get in and ride with me. It will be easier getting into the gate."

As we were about to pulled over, I stopped and texted her that I wanted her on the edge of her bed on all fours. As expected she texted back her compliance.

When we got to the gate, I punched in the code went inside and backed my truck into the furthest parking space. I pulled out a joint for Chris and I to smoke. I knew she would be expecting me to walk in within a minute or two once I came in the gate. I knew she would be getting more and more nervous as the time passed. After about ten minutes I turned my truck off, and we made our way upstairs to the 2nd floor.

Music played inside the house. I walked toward her bedroom door to see her in the position that I instructed her to be in. I could see her pussy pulsating and glistening from her wetness, she was anticipating what I had in store for her. I walked back into the kitchen and put my keys and my phone on the table. Chris put his keys and phone next to mind.

When we both walked into the bedroom, I smacked her ass, she moaned as she arched her back. I got undressed, walked over to the bed, and positioned my cock inches from her mouth. I grabbed her by the hair and she instantly opened her mouth and licked her lips knowing she was going to have a mouth full. With one hand she reached out and grabbed my cock and started to jack me off. I was so hard as I watched her take my dick halfway down until she started to choke. She pushed down deeper; her choking got louder until she pulled her head back to fill her lungs with air. Then she forcibly shoved it back down her throat again.

I signaled for Chris to start fucking her from behind. At that very moment I pushed my dick deeper down her throat. I could feel her trying to scream with pleasure when Chris entered her from behind. Her nails started to dig into my legs, and she sucked my cock faster, taking it deeper down her throat.

He started to fuck her hard and fast. She pulled my dick out of her mouth and started to jack me off. I knew she was about to cum. Just before she began to cum, I started fucking her face. It only took me a short time before I started to cum down her throat. I could feel my cum filling her mouth and I could feel when she decided to swallow the whole load.

I slid off the bed and walked over to the dresser and grabbed a condom and slipped it on. By this time Chris had made his way to the bed and put his thick cock in her mouth. I slipped my dick inside of her and I saw her back dipped down welcoming a familiar cock. I knew she was stretched out, because Chris cock was much thicker than mine, but I was much longer than he was. I also knew that he had hit her deep enough to put her in a subspace zone, it takes a lot to get her into this zone.

Subspace is when you cum so much and so uncontrollably that you lose all control of your body, almost an out-of-body experience. It is also a mixture of pain, mixed with extreme pleasure.

Once I started to fuck her, I knew just how to make her cum and how to make her cum fast and often. She and I have had many long talks on the things she liked and the things she like to have done to her. I put the first inches of my cock inside of her. In, out, in, out, but with a steady pace until I start to feel her pussy tighten around my hard cock. I went deeper, faster, but always with a constant pace. I looked at her to make sure she had her blindfold on, and she was worshipping the dick in front of her. Without warning to her I put all 10 inches of my cock inside of her and she instantly started to cum. I was giving her long, deep, hard thrust. I could feel my nuts hitting her clit, I could feel her cum squirting on me. I continued to fuck her; she pulled my friends cock out of her mouth to catch her breath. I started to rub my thumb in a circular motion on her asshole knowing that I was waiting for the right moment to enter her with my thumb.

She knew at that moment I had plans to use all of her. She knew that her night was about to get so much more intense. She relaxed more and my thumb slipped right inside of her. I pulled my cock out of her pussy and replaced the used condom

with a fresh one. I put more lube on my cock and made sure it was nice and hard for her. I put the tip in her ass, I did this so she could control how much went inside of her, and I want her to think she was in control of this part.
She inched back and forward until all 10 inches of my hard cock was inside of her.

I noticed laying on the bed next to her was her sex wand. I grabbed it, turned it on and placed it under her on her clit. I leaned over and told her to hold it there and not to move it under any circumstance. I grabbed her hips and pulled her closer as I went deeper. I didn't want to fuck her too hard right now, not because I didn't want to hurt her.

After a few more minutes of me inside of her ass, I start to slide to the right to get off the bed, I pulled my cock out of her and walked into the bathroom and started to shower off a little. When I turned the shower off, I could hear her and my homeboy going at it. I knew there was fucking going on because she was screaming that she was about to cum again. To my pleasure she still had her blindfold over her eyes. I walked over to the bed and told her to ride my cock, I pulled her closer to me which exposed her ass to him. He climbed onto the bed and entered her while I was still inside of her.

"Oh my God there's two cocks inside of me at the same time! I'm fucking cumming already. Please don't stop, please don't stop. Oh my God! Thank you, Sir! Y'all are fucking me so fucking good right now. I can't believe this is actually happening right now," she said between orgasms.

I reached up and grabbed her by the neck and started to squeeze harder and harder. She started to tap my arm, but I didn't stop. I looked her in the eyes, and they were filled with lust and pleasure. She smiled and passed out. We started to fuck her limp body harder and faster.

A few second later she woke up.

"Holy fuck y'all are still fucking me! I'm about to cum again!"

We all starting to cum at the same time, once he pulled his cock out of her she collapsed onto me and rolled off me onto her back. I got off the bed and stood up and my boy was locked in on her.

"I'm not done with you yet. I have to cum one more time."

I walked back into the bathroom to wipe off again and started to get dressed. I went into the kitchen and grabbed my phone to check if I had any messages or missed calls. *Perfect!* No missed calls.

When I walked back into the bedroom to get my shoes they were still fucking. Minutes later he was cumming all over her.

My friend stood up and started to get dressed as she laid there for a few second to recompose herself. I gave her a wet towel so she could wipe the cum off her face, then reached over and pulled her blindfold off her face and when she saw me, she had the biggest smile on her face.

"This is my friend Chris." She looked at him and smiled.

"Well it was a pleasure to meet Chris. I hope you enjoyed yourself just ask much as I did."

We exchanged small talk before Chris, and I walked out of her apartment. I stopped at the door.

"Clean yourself, I'm not done with you and I want you posted up like a good whore when I get back."

"Yes sir."

Chapter 10

Lately I had been playing on this swingers' site a lot more than normal and it had been tons of fun. I was so busy with that I didn't have time to meet up with anyone else. I did receive a text from Shannon telling me how great and unexpected her surprise was.

She texted, "Thomas, wow, what a great Christmas gift."

I replied, "Well, I was so glad that I could put a smile on your face. I knew you wouldn't expect it, so I was like, fuck it tonight is the perfect time to do it."

"Oh it was perfect, and the blindfold took one of my senses away and that turned me on, but when you said to put earbuds in so I wouldn't know when you were coming I was almost in overload. I can usually time how long it takes for you to get into my place after I buzz you in, but you made me wait so much longer. I actually came from waiting with so much anticipation. That was really one of the hottest things I have ever had done to me. Shit, I even told my home girl about it," she said with excitement.

I laughed reading it and texted back, "Oh yea! And what did she say about?"

"She said I should write it down. Do you want to read it?" she asked.

"Hell yes, I sure do. Send it to my email address. You still have it right?" I asked.

"Yes, I'll send it now. Okay…sent," she said.

I went to get my laptop and pulled up my email and there it was titled 'The Gift That Kept Cumming.' I laughed and thought that was actually a really good title. I rolled a joint and laid across my bed and began reading:

Have you ever received a gift that was so completely unexpected that you were humbled by the act?

This Christmas was like any other Christmas...uneventful. I spent time with family and friends, in anticipation of time with a 'friend' that was able to get away for a couple hours. I was excited to spend some playtime with Him. He is someone that recently surprised me in several ways. He is both respectful of boundaries and someone that pushes them hard. We've spent some time together, in both playtime and deep discussions on writing techniques and BDSM book ideas. So, when we planned a scenario playtime on Christmas day, I was extremely excited to have some fun.

Doing as instructed, I was 'posted' up and ready for Him. I was on my knees with a grip on the edge of the mattress. For me, black, 6-inch heels with diamond studs and sharp spikes accented with a black see through nighty was the outfit for the evening. "No panties needed tonight," he playfully texted earlier in the day.

My ass was pointed toward the ceiling, as if there is a piece of twine wrapped around my clit pulling it up toward the heavens. Exposing not only my ass but my very moist lips. The juices served as a stream of enticing aroma and lubrication. My right cheek bone was plastered on the bed, baring my upper body weight. And as expected, my arms reached around parted thighs and gripped my ass cheeks, spreading them apart. Welcoming Him to taste, touch, use or abuse as He desires.

All of this runs through my head as I am doing just that. I eagerly awaited the man that has a way of taking over my soul. It is as if a switch is turned on when he is near. I feel sexy, sensual, successful; I feel the need to show Him that He is a fine specimen of a warrior, conqueror, and gentle heart in need of just what I have to offer. And in return, I get the chance to experience sexual pleasures otherwise out of my reach.

I've been told to be posted on the bed with a blindfold on and ear buds in. This is the first time He has requested the blindfold, but we have discussed everything He asked of me ahead of time. I feel comfortable enough that He understands my limits and will push them as hard as I permit and then just a little more. The only problem I truly have with the blindfold is the technology aspect. I do not want pictures or video taken without my knowledge. But I feel comfortable enough that I am okay with the request. The ear buds play the music that fills the house in surround sound. The melodies overcome any possibility of another sound penetrating the world being created. The music steals the knowledge of what is going on around me. My body has no choice but to take in the tones and energies of the beat. I see nothing in the darkness but swirls of color filling the space creating the idea of endless possibilities; realizing my vulnerability, the peace from within takes over. This is my chance to be a success, to satisfy, to obey, to be His desire; to be pleasured beyond comprehension. And, to simply have a most memorable experience. I am both secretively giddy with the excitement of a playdate and the shear knowledge of past experiences. He has asked things of me that I would have said no way, never, but...

I feel the A/C turn on and the cool breeze dances across my wet folds exposed because of my position. I know he is within 10 minutes of arriving. I have accepted his entrance at the gate. The ring alerting me of his arrival, almost dropped me to my knees. I quickly accepted the call and punched 9 opening the gate. Just enough time to potty, freshen up and position myself as instructed. I take a quick drink, knowing it will be my last for a while. I potty and make my way back to the bed. I pull my blindfold over my eyes which helps to create a world of mystery, fear, anticipation, and complete child-like excitement. The earbuds are the final touch to controlling most of my senses. This music play list moves from a 'seductive slow grinding tease' to an 'edgy, playful tone', adding a good 'fuck me hard, and know I'm boss' regiment. Climbing up on the bed, I rocked back on my heels, on the edge of the mattress so that when I fell forward, exposing my pussy, my absolute trust would be apparent.

I am not cuffed but I might as well have been. You could not have pried me away from that spot for any amount of money. The anticipation building has my body quivering in areas that I never realized could move in such an involuntary way. Moisture took over the opening of my throbbing canal. I feel the excitement run over the tip of my clit as a cool drop released and fell. With no sight, controlled sound, and a comfortable temperature for my almost naked body, my eagerness to please Him grew. With every second awaiting His arrival in this posted position, my hunger grew. A feeling much like, I could only imagine, a wild animal experiences just before they pounce.

I never really know what to expect with each visit. Each one has been unique in a naughty or dominate way. I know He will have me worship His cock with my throat. This excites me very much because I have prepared. I have limited my solid food intake for most of the day. I want Him to enjoy my throat without the thought of a possible mess that would not be fun to clean up. Lol That's really more for my comfort level. I do know He has enjoyed humiliating me and making me release my lunch. I do crave his power and willingness to take what He desires.

I start to get a bit anxious and wiggle to relieve the tension building. The music that fills my everything at this moment is a playful tune that welcomes movement or even a tap of the foot. Without any warning there was a fast, hard and stinging slap on my right ass cheek. Why I wasn't expecting it, I will never know. Then the second came; this time on the left cheek. I jumped, pulling away quickly. Then just as quickly, I reposted myself in the position he requested; on my knees, on the edge of the bed with my ass in the air and my face on the bed, knowing this would please Him. A couple more slaps to announce his dominance and the start of our time together. Oh, how I crave, need and must have this time. I thanked him for each slap that left His mark letting Him know how much I appreciate the time and energy it takes to be the man He is for me.

I am like a puppy greeting his master after a long day of work. He brought His cock around to my mouth, leaving me posted and exposed. Grabbing my hands and pulling them by his sides, I searched for His cock with only my mouth. Using my tongue as a tool of exploration; sucking and licking on anything that came close to my lips until success was accomplished. Drawing the head into my mouth with an eagerness of a newborn babe. Making the connection, as if my life depended on it.

Filling my mouth then my throat with His cock was both exciting and orgasmic. Him pulling my arms made His cock push past the 'normal' depths of my throat and into a chamber that felt was virgin territory. He pulled harder and held His cock so deep inside me. There was no way to think of anything else in the world having greater value than the ecstasy this act gave. This was a moment that gave me the feeling of complete submission. I can't breathe. I can't see. The only thing I smell is His warm scent of lust. His juices are running down my throat. I surrender to His control of my everything at this moment. The moisture between my legs became a gushing mess that was my reward for being a good girl.

...I thought the amazing orgasm was my reward for being a good girl. Just as I released and let go, allowing the juices free, I gasped so hard from the pain. This sudden movement pulled His cock even deeper into my throat. Simultaneously, I was firmly grabbed on both hips by two quite unexpected strong hands and a thick cock was shoved into my very wet pussy. I was absolutely on sensory overload in every shape of the word. The scene He created by using sensory deprivation and then taking my throat and making me cum was completely over the top fulfilling but with this addition I am not sure I can process what was happening. I seemed to be in a state of euphoric confusion. He released me off of His cock allowing me to breathe and gasp from the oversize cock plunging into my pussy hard and fast. He quickly pulls me back onto his cock saying, "You like that big black cock in your pussy, you little white whore?" I knew I could not respond at the moment but knew exactly what I would say when I got the chance to breathe again. "Yes Sir!" He continued to fuck my throat; holding me on him just long enough for me to gag and spit. Now I'm a mess. I'm His nasty little whore. The pounding continues. Then they both pull away from me, leaving me exposed on both ends and not knowing what was coming next. I am well trained and know that I am expected to repost every time I am free of His touch. I am to get ready for whatever he has next for me. I wiggle back to the original spot on the bed and take that imaginary twine and pull my clit toward the ceiling, arching my back as deep as I can possibly go, exposing everything for His use and inspection. I have no idea what is happening around me. Are they talking? Planning?

Leaving? Finished with me? Everything ran through my head in that split second.

The music thundering through the earbuds was all encompassing, not allowing me to hear anything being said. I can't see where they are. My thoughts run to scary, exciting, fun, and nasty corners of my mind. Before I could catch my breath completely, the unfamiliar cock that was just in my pussy is now in my face. The smell of latex is apparent. He takes no time with niceties as he shoves his thick cock in my mouth while also pinning my hands beneath him. I work his cock with my mouth and tongue the best I can. His cock is thicker than is comfortable in an open mouth. I'm grateful he works my head up and down his cock but never pushed to the depths that my Sir pushes me. I enjoy the long strokes, taking his cock and head in and out of my mouth. Only minutes passed before He came behind me. I could tell he had taken the time to put a condom on before penetrating me. As I'm sucking this thick cock, He begins rubbing and pushing on my asshole. I immediately tense up. Again, why I didn't expect this is beyond me but He wanted to show me who owned this 'little white whore'.

He worked His way into my ass quickly. I could only imagine Him saying, "Relax and take this black cock, you little white whore." So, since I couldn't hear, I must not have complied with the speed he expected. He started slapping my ass hard, on both sides until I relaxed and pushed back on His cock. He finally stopped slapping when I took the whole thing in my ass. He is very long.

Now I have a thick, unfamiliar cock in my throat and a long, powerful cock in my ass. The orgasms grew quickly and released just as fast; building to a climax that leaves you empty. Just as the warm liquid becomes something unstoppable they both pull off of me again. It felt like a band aid made from Duct Tape is ripped from the tenderest of spots. Trying to catch my breath and repost as quickly as I can, my limbs move slower than I hoped. I was assisted with eager hands putting my ass back where it belongs and pushing my face down on the bed. I assume they have changed places again. I began rooting around for His cock. I crave the taste of His juices. I find it and go to town; sucking with great eagerness. He grabs my face, slowing me down. He reaches around and takes out my earbuds. The emptiness is overwhelming. I could still hear the music but off in the distance. But now, I could hear His moans as I took his cock in my mouth leaving it wet and eager for more. What a sense of tranquility, to hear His movements, His excitement. He tells me to climb up on His cock and ride him. I do as instructed, enjoying the freedom to move as I want.

I forgot there was someone else in the room. The emptiness and tranquility came to a halt when I felt that big THICK black cock wanting to enter my ass. Holy Shit!! This can't happen. He grabs my hips pulling me to him. Not letting me get away. He grabs me by my face using both hands to steady me and says, in a soft but serious tone, "you will take that big thick black cock in your ass and my cock in your pussy! Do you understand?" Again, the only response I could muster was, "Yes Sir!" He almost growled, "This is what you wanted, wasn't it?" Again, my only response was, "Yes Sir!" "Then, take that thick ass cock for Me!" which melted my resolve. With each word, His cock pushes in and out of my naturally well lubed pussy. "But before we do that, you are going to take them both in your pussy," came a command that held both utter tenderness and a lethal edge if disobeyed.

Is this even physically possible? Will I be torn? Will this please Him? My thoughts ran wild but the only thing I could say was, "Yes Sir! Please Sir." He is taking possession. He owns me. I was going to do this. Still not being able to see was happening around me, I was placed in a way that exposed both pockets of entrance. Riding atop and bent forward, he tried to push the head of his dick into the already overfilled hole. It wasn't happening. "OK, let's stop," He said with a level of defeat. I could hear the disappointment. I jumped to attention, like a soldier being called forth to complete a top-secret mission. "No Sir! Please, let me try again. I can make it work. Please Sir. Let's try again?" I begged.

I'm sure, truth be told, I didn't have to beg so hard for such a request. But, I did not want Him disappointed in any way. I rocked forward on His cock as far as I could bringing the slit up and open at the top. He pushed. I wiggled until the thick tip entered the wetness. I pushed back taking both cocks into my pussy. The pain was a welcomed fullness that quickly brought me to gushing orgasms. Knowing my energy level was depleting quickly, the second cock in my pussy slipped out of the vice and searched for my ass.

He takes my face in His hands again, reminding me to breathe and that I was going to take both of these big black cocks again. Leaning into Him, I expose my ass for this thick cock. 'I can do anything I choose to do, and I choose to please Him' I calmly repeat in my mind. "Yes Sir! Please fill me up with a cock in my ass and pussy Sir!" I ramble. He enters my ass sweetly with lube as needed. They both stroked slowly, in and out of me. He was using neither determined force nor depth, but the slide of the two heads inside me gliding against the same walls took over. Every nerve ending in my body shut down in order to allow my lady parts to bask in the overpowering, humbling, torturous toppling. The greediness overtook the new thick cock. He wanted my ass hard and fast.

I'm extremely grateful he applied lube as needed but it didn't take long, he was fucking my ass so hard with the intension to hit rock bottom. My Sir pulled away leaving me to be more flexible and able to move to a position that opened me up so that his thick cock bottomed out with every slamming stroke. He was fucking me with long and extremely fast strokes. I'm screaming in pure ecstasy. He puts His hand over my mouth telling me, "Shut the fuck up, you nasty ass whore." The pain was overpowered by the pleasure and pure satisfaction of accomplishment. I could not believe I was able to take him but I did. I did it for Him. He will be happy with me. He continued to pound me harder and harder. I knew this had to end soon. I would not be able to physically handle it much more. The pleasure and pain scale was tipping. I begged, "Please cum in my ass! Please!!!" I repeated the mantra on both exhalations and inhalation when either was even possible. I not sure if it was even comprehensible but the message was plain and clear. With the deepest of groans, he pulled out, freed his cock and released his load on my back. It covered me from the top of my head to the crack of my ass. The cool stream gathered, quickly drying in place. A true mark of a good whore.

Void of his cock, I relaxed, and the gush was unstoppable. I came with a tenderness of appreciation. Enjoying the moment and relished the lack of intrusion in my ass. One breath then two and His hands are on my hips, pulling me to His newly wrapped hard cock. His cock hit my ass and I begged, "Please!!! Sir!! Not my ass Sir!! Please!!!" He smacked my ass, signaling for me to repost and display my pussy for Him. I wanted to disobey. No, not really. I wanted to want to disobey. But, I wanted to obey and do as I was told. I wanted to give or take whatever He needed from me. With my ass still on fire from the pounding it just took and my pussy soaking wet, they both belonged to Him. I slowly moved into position, exposing my ass and pussy for His use. He slapped my ass with his cock then with the greatest of vigor He took my pussy hard and fast. Lifting one leg over His shoulder and pinning the other straight down, opening me up extremely wide. Able to angle just right, He hit the deepest of caverns, busting through walls getting there. I began the begging again. "Please, cum Sir... Please!" with not much more than a whisper. He pushed deeper and deeper making me cum to pure exhaustion, looking me in the eye knowing the orgasms continue under His control. He sees it in my eyes, He knows, I am there. He pulls out dispersing proof of His satisfaction all over my tits, face and mouth. He smeared it all over my face, scooping it into my mouth. "You are such a good dirty little whore. Are you my little white whore?" This time the standard response was more like begging, "Yes Sir?" He gives my tits a little slap and gets up off of me.

I am slow to stand. My limbs aren't cooperating with my thoughts very well. He is slipping on underwear and a tank. Damn He is tall, strong standing, and extremely perceptive. As I get to my feet, I look up and try to express myself by saying, "Thank you so much," again, almost a whisper. He looks at me and points behind me, "This is my homeboy, Chris." I spin around, I forgot there was someone else in the room. Chris is sitting there in a high-backed office chair. He looks to be admiring the scene with great thought. When I turn around, I see a smile grow on his face, a mile long. I felt like a little girl that was just caught being naughty by her daddy. But quickly remembered what he just did to my ass. I almost giggled, "Hi Chris. Nice to meet you. Thank you. That was amazing." He didn't even speak to me. He just shook his head and said, "When you told me she was the best, I didn't believe you. Damn man, where did you find her? And, I didn't think you were getting me a Christmas gift..." He continued shaking his head mumbling. "One of my friends bought me a car and another has bought me a motorcycle, but damn man. You out did them both!!" We all laughed and enjoyed a tender moment of flattery and complete satisfaction. I thanked them both again, knowing they were the ones that felt like doing the thanking.

I was instructed to shower and clean up. He was going to walk Chris out and would be back in about 10 minutes. Fresh and clean but extremely sore I was eager to talk about this and thank Him for making this happen. I was sipping a much-needed drink when He walked in. I turned and without a word I knew He was not finished with me. He nodded in the direction of the bedroom. I had just opened my mouth to say, "OMG, Thank you soooo much!" but was stopped with nothing more than a nod. The second His head tilted in the direction of the spot where He just surprised me, I nearly dropped my drink and leapt up and into position. Posted up on the bed with my ass in the air and my face on the bed.

I could hear Him moving around behind me putting on a condom. I am so raw, my pussy sore and my ass still on fire. Without a word, I get about 10 slaps to the ass. Each one harder than the last, alternating between the cheeks. "Thank you, Sir," I gasp. He then took my hips in both hands and pull me back on Him with a might thrust. Completely and totally unexpected He filled my ass. With the drive of a jealous lover, He took my ass again and again. "Are you my little white whore? Will you fuck any cock I bring you? Can I fuck this ass anytime I want to? This is my ass, isn't it? This is my pussy, isn't it? You will fuck any cock I tell you to!" The words are coming out between thrusts of different depths. But each thrust is deeper than the last and harder than the last. Very deliberate strokes. Imprinting a message in my mind and heart. He owns me... "Yes sir... yes sir..."

I knew better than to beg for Him to cum this time. This was His time. He was doing exactly as He desired. He wanted to make sure I understood. He is the one that made this happen. He controls this level of pleasure. He will inflict the pain needed to get me there. He slammed His cock in my ass harder and faster than I ever thought possible. Unable to breathe, I ride the pain, knowing it will stop soon. The rhythm became harder, longer, and slower. Each thrust pulling every ounce of His energy clear from His soul. His breath leaving His body in a whoosh, emptying His lungs to zero capacity. Draining Him of everything. Rolling over He pulls my face to His cock saying, "Swallow My cum you little white nasty ass whore." I eagerly opened my mouth to take it all in. It hit my forehead, in my nose, hair and ended in my mouth. His hand just under my chin pushing it shut, giving the silent command to swallow. I do as instructed. Then He takes His hand and wipes His juices all over my face, down my chest and over my tits. "Now, let's chat about the chapters you were told to read this week," He said with a satisfied grin.

"As you wish Sir," as my lips turn upward, unable to hide the giddy pleasure filling me up from within. I wiped my eyes. Work my way to a comfortable seating position. He gave me a towel and made sure I was OK. I sat on the bed with my legs spread wide open to allow the cool breeze to refresh my thoroughly used lady parts. He served me a drink and ask if there is anything I need. I'm thinking, You just gave me a winning lottery ticket and you want to still ask what you can give? I say, "No thank you, I'm in a good place right now." But He found a way to give me something I didn't realize I needed.

He was sitting in the chair next to the bed. He sweetly reached over and took my hand. Caressing and playfully twirling my fingers as we recovered together, laughing and recalling moments of surprise, the pleasures and the lovely pains. We spoke of work, life and writing ideas. We discussed new limits that can be toyed with and ones that can be pushed even harder in future play sessions. Respectful conversation with unspoken boundaries about fulfilling fantasies and desires of the heart can be more rewarding than the act itself at times. Completely surprised, He gave me an unexpected gift that kept *cumming back for more and more, making sure I got just what I wanted for Christmas this year. He gave me a bit of Himself.*

After Thoughts...

Walking Him to the door, the energy seems to be collapsing from within. A wave of fresh air fills my lungs as I breath Him in. With a tender kiss and the warmest of hugs, He leaves me to my thoughts. Collapsing on the bed from pure exhaustion and shock at what had just transpired. I can't stop the smile from spreading in a mischievous way. My heart fills as if it is floating amongst the clouds. I can't believe what just happened. I have dreamed, fantasized, and even tried to create this on my own, but tonight, it really happened.

The anticipation of His visit was the same as always, energetic, and full of the unknown excitement. We have talked in length about fantasies and limits that are fun and others that are deal breakers. He has proven, in the past, to pull sporadically from our combined repertoire of sexual experiences and intrigues. This skill alone is greatly valued when exploring sexual fantasies or adventures of any kind. I find excitement in being able to help someone else fulfill fantasies. Knowing that I am giving them something that no one else could or would, absolutely brings me a level of accomplishment that feels like the greatest of prides.

I know that might sound like I have a low self-esteem but I'm not sure that is what it is... I guess anyone could argue that point from a million angles. I choose to do what I enjoy and let others judge as they like. I am a most unusual type of happy when I am a submissive. So, as long as I am safe, I should do exactly what I enjoy. And, I am very appreciative of the ones that are able to bring me to this point of contentment. I saw a shirt the other day that said, "Do what you enjoy and do it often!"

The act itself had both ups and downs of energy levels, releases, pain and pleasure. The moment I realized there was someone else in the room, bolts of electricity shot from his hands throughout my entire body. The fact that he caught me completely off guard with this addition was like a slap in the face. Every nerve ending in my body woke up and begged for attention. I wasn't able to hear a thing, so the build-up was nonexistence. Every touch, smell, taste was immediate and erotic. I didn't need to hear a word to understand His needs, wants or desires. He placed me exactly where He wanted me and how He wanted me. He took what he wanted, and I gave everything I could give in order for him to be completely satisfied. This satisfaction created a mutual eagerness.

My mind moves from position to position and pains to pleasures. Before I know it, I wake to the warm sun breaking through the blinds and the knowledge of what had happen the night before. My eyes felt crusty and difficult to open, and my face felt tight. Remembering His hand spreading His cum all over my face brought the widest of grins. I look around at the mess. Now when someone asks my how my Christmas was, all I can do is grin and say, "I had a most amazing Christmas!"

I closed the email. *Holy fuck that was hot.* I closed my laptop and started planning my trip up to Philly to see my home.

Chapter 11

I was laying on my bed and decided to visit this adult website to see if I could find some future playmates. I scrolled down until I saw an event that I wanted to go to in Philly. I opened the event details to read about the group. Once I read the details, I decided that I would open the guest list to see if it was worth my time. I strolled through the list until I came up to a picture of this single female profile and for some reason I was so drawn to this picture. It was simple, classy, and sexy. It was only a picture of her black suede heel, her seemingly long strong legs and her black cocktail dress. I just needed to read more about her. I was hoping she was more than just legs and a pussy. Once I open the profile I begun reading and it was a simple disclaimer with three stars on each side:

I don't check my instant messages

I like that she seems like a no-bullshit type of girl. I read on liking everything I read. I smiled because she told you everything she wanted in a man. And the last thing she wrote in her profile was, 'I can say I'm pretty fucking awesome, but come find out for yourself.' So, I had to send her a message and within an hour she replied:

Me: If you are that fucking awesome, I must meet you...lol... good morning.

Her: Lol...Good morning. Your profile made me laugh with that athletic comment??

Me: Lol...thanks, it gets old when you go to meet a couple or female and the pictures are 10 years old and they are overweight, talking about "I only want fit men"...I'm like well hell baby-girl you have to be fit, too...lol How was your weekend?

Her: I can imagine. It's the same how guys post the pic with the best angle to make their dick look bigger lol...I'm kidding. My weekend was good, just family stuff. How was yours? Wait, when I looked at your profile it said Florida sometimes now it says Allentown. Where ya from?

Me: Lol...I live in Florida but I'm going to be in Allentown from Wednesday to Sunday. How far from Allentown are you?

Her: I'm around an hour and half from Allentown.

Me: I think we should meet up for a few drinks...if you are ok with that. Can I see a picture of your face? Your ink is so fucking sexy.

Her: I like your pics. We can do that. What you in Allentown for? Work or pleasure?

Me: If I get my hands on you PURE PLEASURE lol ...no, my really good friend lives up there so I'm flying up to see him for few days. I'm looking forward to it. I'm taking a bus to D.C., never been to those places.

Her: I am thinking about going to a club next Friday, might meet there, too, if a drink doesn't work. Believe it or not, I haven't seen DC either and I been living around here for 15 years.
Me: Wait, what but you live right there? lol I understand I live 20 minutes from Disney and I've never been there. How's that club for single men?

Her: I'm guessing you don't have kids. Yea, I been to Disney twice. That's more than enough tho. Last time was last year I said to my son remember this bc I ain't coming again...lol. How is pleasure garden for single guys...it depends... pleasure garden is a hit or miss even for single girls, sometimes it's packed sometimes it dead.

Me: I have 3 kids. I hope it's good when I go. How long have you been in the lifestyle?

Her: On and off for 5 years. But I am not regularly active and every so often I get bored with it and don't do anything for months and months. Most in the lifestyle are after a quick fuck and that bores me. I am in an open marriage, mostly see vanilla guys when I step out. What about you?

Me: 3 years on and off mostly off....lol.....I go to a few house parties but I rarely if ever play at house parties I feel like you have to put on a show and I'm not big into that.....I like to get to know the person.

Her: I hate house parties. There's so much pressure to play. I like clubs better, different atmosphere, you drink you dance you hang out, and if you feel like playing you play. House parties are like a bunch of horny desperate people who never get laid...and as you can see, I am a woman with strong opinions, lmao...

Me: Lol...strong is putting it mildly...lol....but I like it....so what are you into if you don't mind me asking?

Her: Haha, I've had a few bad experiences. Mostly with women. For some reason women think that it's okay to start touching and grabbing you because you are at a party and list yourself as bi. Guys would never get away with that shit. I like a strong assertive male with a dirty mouth. A very dirty mouth lol...What about you?

Me: Yummmmmmm I like dirty...dirty is great.

Her: I like interracial dirty talk the most...lol

Me: Explain that one to me. I know what I think you are saying but I just want to be clear.

Her: Black dick/white slut etc. I like to be treated dirty in bed.

Me: We should get along really good. lol

Her: Yea...or bad, lol...Are you into that?

Me: You like race play....I'm game for anything...well almost, I don't do bi anything. lol

Her: I mean worst names and adjectives than the examples I gave lol. Nothing too crazy.
Me: Lol...I love it...I love that type of talk and I am kinda rough too

Her: I don't like quiet sex or soft sex all the time. A man's gotta treat me dirty in bed, he can be a gentleman outside of bed lmao

Me: My dick getting hard thinking about the fun I can have with you. Just thinking about covering you with my cum...

Her: I haven't had anyone use the N word in bed in years. You won't believe how many men are shy or have a problem with that kinda talk in bed. The way I see it is, what happens during sex stays there.

Me: So you like using the N word in bed...

Her: Not necessarily use it, but I like hearing it.

Me: That's hot, even with both people saying it.

Her: I think so too. But very few people are into that.

Me: You can call me absolutely anything you want...the dirtier and nastier the better

Her: I like that. How tall are ya?

Me: 6'3" 254 pounds

Her: Damn that's nice!

Me: Lol....thank you sweetheart

Her: Do you enjoy group sex?

Me: I do...not all the time

Her: Yes same here.

Me: You are fucking sexy

Her: Lol you're hotter

Me: ...and dirtier...

Her: Wait who's dirtier me or you?

Me: You are...no I might be.

Her: Yea I have a feeling you are VERY dirty...

Me: When I'm in the mood I'm ALL in.

Her: I should make you in the mood then ????????

Me: I think you should too...good morning beautiful

Her: Good morning handsome

Me: Here's my number, that should make it much easier...407-953-0... and by the way, I'm Thomas.

Her: Pleasure to meet you Thomas, and I'm Jackie. My number is 278-856-78... Call or text me whenever you want babe.

This conversation went on for another week before we sat a time, date, and a location, which was Friday the 19th at 10pm. We talked daily about anything, everything, and sometimes we talked about nothing. I learned all about her likes, her dislikes, how to touch her and get the best response from her body. I learned everything about her that could bring her to the point of pure bliss. I was talking to her and learning to connect with her on an even deeper emotional and spiritual level. We made a true connection. I cared about how her day went, I told her goodnight and good morning. As the date slowly approaches, I found myself playing out different scenarios in my head on how the night could play out. Once Friday night came, I woke up and texted her good morning, and I also wanted to make sure we were still on for the night.

"Good morning beautiful," I texted.

"Good morning handsome! I'm looking forward meeting you. I hope we connect in person like we have over the phone." She replied to me.

"I'm pretty sure we will, I think the connection we have will surly carry over. I have no doubts whatsoever. Beside the worst thing that can happen at this point is that we have become good friends" I said.

"True! Well I have to get up and get my day started I'll text you later babe," she texted.

After I finally got up and started moving around, I got dressed and started rolling a blunt for me and my homeboy. I walked upstairs to the main level of my friend's house. He and his family were already up making breakfast. I just thought to myself what a welcoming and loving household. I felt like I was a part of the family. I looked at him and motion for him to walk onto the back porch. He nodded and headed to the back.

When I opened the back-sliding glass door I could finally understand the true beauty of my surrounding. The air was crisped, clean, and had the prefect chill to the wind. I was in the right place at the right time. This is where God intended for me to be at this very moment in my life. I think we both needed this to get ourselves back into the right mindset for the unknown fight we had ahead of us as friends and now as family.

We sat on the back porch and just talked and laughed for hours. We talked shit about each other, old friends, co-workers, family, kids, and anything and anyone else that came to mind. I have always looked at him as a good friend but at this moment we became family. After another hour we decided to drive down the mountain to eat and maybe try to see a few waterfalls. Once we finished eating lunch, we headed out to the homeless shelter to see his sister. On our way back we stopped at this small spring. It was beautiful; I felt like a little kid seeing something new for the first time.

After taking in the natural beauty of my surrounding, we started back to the house. It was about a 20 min drive up and around the mountain. Once we got back to the house, I went to roll another blunt downstairs and Jon walked upstairs to see his mom. When I finished I waked upstairs to the main level and we walked outside to smoke again. We were only out there for an hour before I told him I had to get ready for to take a nap because I had a 2-hour drive ahead of me if I was going to Philly. As I walked downstairs to lie down and plug my phone up, I got a text.

"Hey handsome! Looks like it going to rain in Philly tonight."

"I see that; it's storming here too, it should clear up by the time I need to leave." I replied.

"So we might be able to meet, I'm still going to go, but I don't know how feel about driving in bad weather," she said.

I laughed and said, "You think a little rain is going to stop me from meeting you. Not a chance in hell. As long as you are planning on going I will be there."

She responded with some heart emojis and said, "See you tonight handsome."

"Okay beautiful, looking forward to seeing you," I said.

I laid down excited, but I was strangely nervous to meet her. As I was lying on the couch my mind started running a thousand miles a minute. I walked out front and smoked the rest of the blunt Jon and I started. I finished and went back to the couch and kicked my feet up. My eyes started to close, and I slowly fell into a deep sleep, a much-needed rest. When I woke up, I rolled over and grabbed my phone to check the time. A two-hour nap was just what I needed. I shower shaved and got dressed. I left an hour early so I could stop to get me some food and a drink. When I finally arrived in Philly I decide to swing by a bar and get something to eat, but a good strong drink might do me some good with my nerves. Once I finished, I made my way to the club to finally meet her.

Once I got there and finally walked inside, I notice a very sexy girl next door type wearing black rimmed glasses and hot red lipstick, by the door. There was also a medium build old guy helping her with collecting money and putting wrists band on people. Once I finished with them, I walked toward a door where there was a doorman that was patting people down. I stepped up and spread my arms out.

He walked up to me and looks up and said," Man you twice my size! I wouldn't be able to stop you from doing what you want to anyway."

I laughed and said, "Naw, homie you good, I'm not about the bullshit. Nice chill relaxing night."

I was there for about 20 minutes before she arrived. I walked through the whole place to see where the best spot to stand so I could see the whole club, but also be able to see the front door. While I was standing there for a few minutes and I could see a couple looking over at me and smiling, so I smiled back. Once I smiled at them the husband stood up and walked to the other side of the club, and this wife walked up to me and introduced herself to me. We talked for a minute before her husband came over. We laughed a little, and as we were talking another female walked past me and grabbed my hand and smiled at me. I returned the smile. The guy and his wife asked if we could chat a little later. Their friend had just arrived. I shook my head yes and they walk away.

Then, out of the corner of my eyes I saw her walk in. I stop what I was doing and watched her for a second as she sped off to the back bathroom. I waited and watched the entrance and about 6 minutes later she reappeared and just stood there. She was tall about 5'9" -5'10" with thick curly brown hair that went down maybe 3 inches below her shoulders. Her hair perfectly curled, not too tight of curls and not too loose. Her skin was perfectly golden, sun-kissed by God. She had on a golden-brown dress with matching heels. The dress was the prefect mix of classy, sexy, with a hint of dirty, it was open over the shoulders and hung down to show the right amount of cleavage. It was totally open which showed off her beautiful artwork on her back. The only place the dress was tight was the bottom around her beautiful thighs.

I could not see her entire face from across the room but from what I could see I was going to be happy. Once she finished taking survey of the room, she started walking toward me. I turned my back so she could approach me first. Then I remembered a conversation we had about her thinking it's hot to have me walk up behind her and whisper something dirty in her ear, so I tilted my head lower. I wanted her to walk pass me so I could walk up behind her and whisper in her ear how I wanted to bend her over the bed and give her all 10 inches of my black cock.

She stopped beside me smiling, and I just had to look up. She was so beautiful. She had thick full lips that I just wanted to bite. Her eyes were something that I could instantly lose myself in. They were almost a greenish-gray color. Her smile was so big it lit up the room. She had big white teeth and little make-up which showed her natural beautiful. I slowly looked at her from the top her head to the tip of her perfect polished toes. I come to a halt looking directly into her eyes and at that very moment the room was quiet, and it was only her and I in that building.

She smiled and said, "Hey handsome."

"Hey beautiful, how are you? Glad you made it," I said.

She said, "I was thinking the same thing."
"You look as beautiful as you looked in your pictures," I said while smiling.

"Well to be honest you are a lot better looking in person. I'm not saying you are a bad looking man, because you are handsome in your pictures. I just think you take bad pictures; you are so much better looking in person. It's usually the other way around." She spoke softly.

"Thanks baby girl! Let go turn in your bottle to the bar," I said.

I made a small walkway for her and followed her lead to the bar. I was watching her walk. She had a fluent stride with no wasted movement. Once we got to the bar she gave the bartender gave her a bottle and quickly turned around and caught me smiling; she smiled back and grabbed her drink turned and said, "Let's go back over to the area you were standing."

She grabbed my hand and gave me a slight pull in her direction, and like a good little boy I followed. We returned to the same place I was previously at and began talking. From the moment we spoke those first words we were inseparable. Our eyes locked on to each other and everyone else quickly faded into the night. We laughed. We smiled. We grew closer, and the sexual tension grew stronger and stronger. I was waiting for the moment that her eyes told me to kiss her, and once that very moment arose, I took advantage of it. My hand was already in the mid-level of her back because this whole time I have lightly been tracing her spine with my fingertips. I slowly moved my hand to her lower back, and I could feel her shiver. I pressed my hand on her lower back and used my other hand to pull her closer. She placed her hand on my chest and ever so lightly pressed her nail into my skin. Our lips melted when they touched. The first kiss wasn't very long, wasn't very wet, wasn't much tongue, but it was the perfect amount of me biting on her lower lips. It was the perfect introduction kiss to what the night would lead to.

She looked at me and said, "Wow! I might be in trouble."

I smiled and said, "Yeah! I think you are too."

With a devilish grin she said, "Okay, but just so you know I'm going to hold you to that."

"I wouldn't expect anything less," I said.

I started talking and I noticed how she was smiling. I could tell she was getting a little buzzed from the drink. She grabbed my hand to kiss my forearms and made her way up and my neck. I could feel her skin starting to warm up. Her soft lips kissed my ear, at that moment she reached down and grabbed my throbbing cock.

"I think we need to find something a little more private."

I grinned at her and said, "I think you are right."

"Let's refill our drinks first I have a feeling we will need it."

I followed her to a private room in the back of the club. Once the doors closed behind me, we put our drinks down and it was like we were magnetically pulled toward each other. This kiss was deep and passionate, sexy, and dirty. As I pulled away a little, I bit down on her bottom lip and I could hear her purred softly.

Once she was finally away from me, she turned around and started crawling onto the bed. When she was halfway on the bed, she turned her head back toward me and licked her lips. I took two steps toward the bed as she faced me. She reached up and started rubbing my hard cock. As she started to unzip my dark blue straight leg jeans, I could see a devilish grin on her face, she bit down on her lips as she looked up at me.

She looked me directly in the eyes and said, "Mmmhmm this cock looks so yummmmm." She then licked my cock from the base to the tip. When she got to the top, she made half of my cock disappear down her throat while she aggressively stoked my throbbing remains. Without warning she tried to get all 10 inches of my cock down. Before she could get it all down, she put her head back and with water and lust in her eyes, she quickly tied her hair up. She took a few deep breaths while still stroking my cock, and with the other hand she grabbed my nuts and put them in her mouth and started sucking.

I could hear her moans of pleasure. My dick was getting harder and harder as she kept stroking. She pulled back and started smiling again. I reached and grabbed her by the neck and deeply kissed her at the same time, pulling her up to her feet. I turned her around and pushed her back on to the bed. I licked my full lips. With the thought of tasting her wet sweet pussy my mouth began to water. It was as if she knew she was about to get the best tongue fucking of her life.

I opened her legs and slowly started licking her soaked pussy. I slowly slipped a finger inside of her wetness while I sucked on her clit. Then I stop. I only wanted to give her a short taste of what she was in for. I moved up kissing each side of her hips, then her stomach and random places on her belly. I then traced my tongue around her naval. The whole while I am running my finger nails up and down her side. Applying the prefect amount of pressure, careful not to leave any marks but enough to make her body quiver with pleasure.

I slowly and methodically made my way to her prefect breast. I traced my tongue between her breast, as my fingers slowly made circles around her hard nipples. Her chest began to rise as she arched her back. Next I take her left nipples into my mouth and start nibbling a little harder than usual, just so she knows it will get harder over time.

"Oh God yes please." She moaned.

I reach up behind her head and grabbed her by her hair and pulled back to expose her neck, and with my other hand I went down to her wet and waiting pussy and enter her with two fingers.

"Oh my God please fuck me please."

I said nothing in reply to her. I just smiled and thought to myself that it was about time for me to feed on her sweetness. So, I retraced my same path to the waiting treasure.
Once I got to her wet pussy I kissed and slipped my tongue inside of her, as her legs automatically spread wider. I started sucking on her clit while I finger fucked her with two fingers.

"Fuck right there. Please don't stop I'm about to cum." She cried.

I sped up the finger fucking deeper and harder. I could feel her that her body was starting to shake. So, I spread her legs wider and started to suck her pussy while rubbing her clit with my fingers. I could taste her cum, which turned me on more.

"Please fuck me right now. Oh my God I can't take it; I can't wait any longer please daddy fuck me!" She was begging.

As I continue to suck on her clit, I reach into my jean pocket and pulled a condom out and put it on, but before I had it completely on, she yelled, "I'm about to fucking cum again." I kept my finger inside of her as I slowly slipped my dick inside of her.

I slowly inched myself deeper and deeper inside of her. With each inch I could feel her nails pressing harder into my back. I was about halfway inside of her when I decided to slowly pull out until the tip of my dick was just inside of her. I then repeat that over, but a little deeper and faster until my whole dick was inside of her. Faster! Harder! Deeper! I felt her nail penetrate my upper back.

She begun to scream, "Don't stop! I'm about to fucking cum. Please don't stop daddy please don't stop."

I whispered in her ear, "You like this big black dick?

She responded, "Yes, Daddy please keep fuck this white pussy. I need that black dick. Fuck I'm cumming."

I pushed myself up and locked my elbows and with one hand I wrapped my fingers around her neck I applied pressure cutting off some of her breathing.

I leaned over until my lips were only inches from her ear and said, "You like that black nigger cock. You like how I'm fucking that white pussy."

I again started fucking her hard and fast and it sent her over the edge. Her eyes rolled behind her head and her body started convulsing uncontrollably. That whet on for about 30 second, and I didn't not stop fucking her I could feel her pussy cumming all over me and that only turned me on more.

She opened her eyes and looked at me and said, "Oh my fucking God you are still fucking me. You are fucking me so fucking good."

I steadily slowed down slipping my ten-inch dick in and out of her. I pulled my dick out of her with her white cream all over. I pulled the condom off and started sucking on her nipples again. Her breathing was fast and shallow.

"What the fuck did you just do to me?"

I look at her and smiled, "Nothing yet! I'm just get started with you!"

"You're fucking crazy. Do you know how sore my pussy is already? I cannot take a beating like that again."

At that moment I flipped her over and put her on her hands and knees and eased my dick back inside of her. As she started to move forward I reached up and grabbed her by her hair with one hand and with the other hand I grabbed her shoulder. I put my knees in between hers so I could spread them as wide as I could. Her arm collapsed and her upper body was touching the bed. I started slipping my dick into her again slowly, but deeper and deeper. Once I got almost all but an inch of my cock inside of her, head popped up off the pillow and started waving side to side.

"I can't take anymore! It's too deep."

I leaned forward and said, "You are going to take all of this nigger dick!"

She started shake her head and said, "Yes sir."

"Yes Sir? Yes sir what?"

"Yes, sir I will take all of your nigger dick."

"That's a good little white whore. You take it all."

After she came five more times I pulled my dick out of her and flipped her back over on her back and ask her if she wanted me to cum all over her.

"Yes please." She smiled.

I entered her again and started fucking her hard and fast. I could feel her nails digging into my back as she yelled, "I want that nigger cum all over me. Please!" At that moment I could feel myself getting to the edge.

"I'm about to cum."

"Yes, please cover me with it."

I pulled my dick out and took the condom off. As I was pulling the condom off, I just explode all over her belly, her chest and her face. Once I finish, I collapsed on the bed beside her. She turned her head to me and smiled.

"My fucking God. You are crazy. I have never in my life been fucked like that."

"But did you cum?" I asked struggling to catch my breath.
"Hell yes, I did! I lost count."

We both laughed as we cleaned ourselves off, and walked out of the room toward the bar for another drink.

Chapter 12

It had been a few weeks since I returned home from Philly. Jackie and I had been texting and talking almost every day. I must be honest I was starting to fall for her. She was beautiful, smart, and really cool to be around. She told me that she would be down in Florida on a special assignment. The crazy thing is I had never gotten an upfront answer on what type of job she had, but I never pressed the issue. I figured when the time was right, she would tell me.

I relived that crazy night in the industrial park a few times, but I always push those thoughts out of my head. But I could not stop thinking about it, I could not get the image of her dead body out of my head. I just always replace those thought with my time in Philly.

What a great time that I had up there. As I drove home, I could not stop smiling from the amazing memories. I made a connection with someone that was stronger than any I had made over the years with people who I knew half my life.

I reach for my radio to change the station, and just as I was about to search for something different I news came on the air asking for help to solve a rape murder case. I leaned back and turned the radio up to try to get a better understanding of what they had. I knew they would release that they found a mens watch in the car. I listened for any tell signs that they had more than they were telling the public. At the end of the news announcement they said that they would be holding a press conference tomorrow at 7pm to give more details and take limited questions.

I thought to myself I must set a reminder to watch this. I was already nervous about what I could possibly lose if anyone found out that I had done something like this. I dialed Michelle's number and ask her if she could come by tomorrow at 6:30pm.

As I expected she showed up early while I was cooking. She pushed the door and walked right in without knocking and just stood there.

"Dammit girl have you ever heard of knocking?" I asked.

She smiled at me and said, "Have you heard of pants?"

I shook my head said, "Pants ewwww, I don't like wearing pants, and beside this is my house weirdo. You lucky I have boxers on."

"Well, if you lock the door I would've had to knock."

"No, you wouldn't! You definitely would not, you would just use the spare key I gave you."
"Well, if you know that, why are you bitching? Beside friends knock on the door, family just walks right in. Anyway, whatever you're cooking smells really good."

"Stuffed pork chops, fried seasoned corn, brussels sprouts with diced onions, chopped bacon, and garlic bread."

"With cheese?"

"Hell yes!"

"So, what did you want me to come here for?"

"They are doing a press conference at 7pm about that girl."

"Oh really!"

"I'm scared."

"Why? If they are doing a news conference, they don't have anything. They have hit a dead end. So, you basically have gotten away with murder."

"Damn when you say it like that, it sounds so wrong."

"REALLY! Fool you killed someone…it is bad. So, have you been thinking about it?"

"I actually have been, but the crazy part is that it isn't with feeling of regrets or shame. The thought of the power takes over my thoughts most days. It wasn't as often, but now it's starting to become more and more. I know I should not have those thoughts, but I like it, I'm starting to crave it. It's starting to feel out of control."

"Are you going to try it again?"

"No! I have thought about it…maybe. No, I can't. I wouldn't be able to live with myself if I did something like that again. The food is done if you want something to eat." I tried to change the subject.

"Hell yes I do, and just in time, the news is coming on."

After I made our plates I walked to the living room to sit down and watch the news.

The Sheriff, Governor, and the District Attorney talked in front of the police station and started giving details of the murder. When the media started asking questions, the Sheriff stopped them and said they brought in the top FBI agents to help with the case. The Sheriff asked for the lead detective to step up to the podium and answer whatever questions she could.

When she started to talk, my heart started to race. I slowly started to look up when I heard an awfully familiar voice. *No! This can't be.*

I reached over to the side table and grabbed my glasses to get a better look. Fuck, it was her! Now I see why she would never give me a straight answer of what type of work she does, and I just got off the phone with her about an hour ago. She told me she worked for the government, but I never thought she was an FBI agent.

"Thomas! Are you okay? You don't look so good right now."

"Do you remember that chick I told you about?"

"Man, are you for real? I hate to break it to you, but you are a hoe. I can't keep up with them."

"Damn for real, it was just a few weeks ago."

"The hairdresser?"

"No!"

"The banker?"

"No!"

"Was it the restaurant manager!?"

"No!" I laughed. "Okay, I might be a hoe. Remember the chick I met online, and we met up at the swinger's club. The one up in Philly!"

"Oh, okay, yeah, I remember. What does she have to do with anything?"

"That's her right there."

"Which one?"

"The one on the news talking right now."

"Holy fuck! Thomas this is not good! This is really bad! You can't see her anymore!"

"I know! I know! But if I don't she will know I'm acting strange."

"She's not going to think anything, but this guy just wanted to fuck and run."

"Okay, but here's the thing. I have been talking to her almost every day. So, she knows this is not a hit it and quit it situation, I like her a lot and I don't want to stop talking to her."
"Well, do you like her more than your freedom? Actually, don't answer that. Whatever you decide to do, just be careful. I know how you get sometimes."

"What the hell does that mean?"

"Never mind!"

She stood up and walked to the kitchen and put her dishes in the sink and asked me if I had any weed. I told her yes and where to find it. We smoked on the back porch and talked for about an hour when my phone started to ring. I reach over and grabbed the phone, it was her, the FBI agent. I thought to myself if I should reply to her.

"Hey babe," she said.

I answered back letting her know I had just seen her on the news, "Hey copper."

"So, you watched the news I see. Sorry I didn't tell you, but how do I just bring that up?"

"No, it's cool, I'm just joking with you."

"Listen, I want to see you. I'm going to be at a hotel at the beach at 10pm tonight. I'm going to leave a key at the front desk."

"Okay see you soon."

"Thomas...10pm don't be late."

"Okay!"

I put the phone down and when I looked up Michelle was staring me in my face. *Shit!* I thought she left. She just stood there without saying a word to me. So, I just stared right back at her, not wanting to be the one to break the eye contact. This was a good old fashion stare down. After a few second it just got a little to creepy for me and I broke the silence.

"What? Why are you staring at me?"

"Because you really are full blown crazy!"

"Why do you say that?"

"Who were you talking to?"

"A lady friend."

"Yeah, that's what I thought. You have a problem, maybe you should leave her alone. Just a thought, be safe that's all I want to say. I'm leaving."

"Thought you left 10 minutes ago!"

"Fuck you! You're a jackass!"

As she walked out, she threw up her middle finger and slammed the door behind her.

"I love you too." I yelled.

I walked into the back room, opened my safe and pulled out a large bag of weed. I sat down and rolled a few blunts to take with me for the night. I lit one and sat down on the bed, the clock read 8:15pm. I sat there for a few minutes deep in thought thinking if I should be doing this. I walked into the bathroom and started the shower so it would be nice and steamy when I was ready to get in, then I finished half of the blunt.

45 minutes later I was out the door and firing up my monster of a car. I sped down the road toward the highway, but the last light caught me. I had my windows down and the radio up listening to Jay-Z. I looked over to my left and saw this young kid pull up next to me. He was in a blacked-out Honda Accord with his girl riding shotgun. It was a pretty nice tricked out car. He started revving his engine. I turned my radio down and leaned out my window a little and looked his car up and down, just to make sure I was seeing what I was seeing. I revved my engine to full throttle. I looked out at him again, laughed, turned my radio back on, and rolled my window up. The light turned green and he shot off like he was

in a hurry to get somewhere. About a quarter mile down the road I saw him get on the highway, going the same direction that I was going. I thought to myself, *what the hell why not, let's have a little fun with him.*

I pulled up beside him on the highway, let my window down, looked at him, and gave him the head nod to let him know I was down. Again, he floored it and sped off. I followed him for about two miles: 70, 80, 100, 110. I put my blinker on and got into the lane next to him and waved bye to him. I dropped my car from 6th gear to 5th, bringing to life all 717 horses I had under the hood. Once I dropped gears the Charger's ghost engine roared to life and peeled out going 110. I picked up speed 120, 130, 140, and it still had more but I saw him fading in the distance and my exit was quickly coming up. I put my turn signal on so I could exit the highway…they followed me to the gas station.

I got out the car, walked inside to get a box of condoms, and fill my gas tank up. As I walked out, he was parked at the next pump. Him and his girl was standing outside his car waiting for me.

"Bro what the hell do you have under the hood?"

"Not much! Stock everything," as I laughed.

"Bullshit!"

"Maybe, maybe not, but you will never know. But I do like your car, it's really cute."

"That's fucked up, bro."

I got in my car, looked in the seat next to me and saw his girl had dropped her number in my ride. I looked up and she was smiling at me, so I returned the smile. I looked at the number again, then looked back at her and threw the number out of the window. She didn't look a day over 17. Thanks but no thanks. I pulled off and headed to my destination.

After about 20 minutes I turned into the self-parking area of the hotel. I walked to the front desk and ask the front desk person if there was a key left for Thomas. She looked at me, smiled, and asked to see my ID. Once she gave me the key card and room number, I started to make my way up to the penthouse of the hotel.

When I walked inside, I was taken aback by the amazing view of the city. I started making my way toward the window, which was floor to ceiling. I had walked down the three steps halfway across the foyer when I heard her say, "Excuse me, dinner is served." I stopped, and slowly turned towards her voice.

She was sitting on a silver platter with a white cloth napkin laid across her belly. On one side of her there was a knife and a fork on the other. She was wearing a pair of red stilettos and nothing else. I walked over to the table, pulled the chair out and took a seat. I grabbed the napkin off her stomach and tucked it in my collar. I didn't want my new shirt to get dirty and I knew this meal would be good and messy.

I leaned forward and took a long, slow lick of her sweet pussy. Once I got to the hood of her clit, I started to suck for a second or two before coming up for air.

"My compliments to the Chef." I smiled

"I'll be sure to pass on the message." She returned the smile with a sexy grin.

I lowered my head and started biting and kissing on the inside of her knee leaving a trail of light kisses to her wet warm pussy. As I slowly crossed over her wetness, I let my tongue gently brush over her pussy. Her body shivered, as she exhaled. I gave her right inner thigh the attention it deserved, biting, licking, and sucking. I could hear her breathing increase. Running my finger softly up and down her sweet wet pussy, I slowly slipped one inside of her, then the other. I sped up and she grabbed the edge of the table. I knew she was about to cum, so I slowed down to a crawl.

I stood up and walked over to her right side and aggressively started biting and sucking on her breast. My finger was still slowly poking in and out of her, faster and faster! I arched her back and tilted her head, and at that very moment I knew she was right where I needed her. I stopped sucking on her tits and stood upright, I rotated my fingers upward, bent them in the form of a hook to make sure I was hitting the g-spot in the right place with the perfect amount of pressure. I felt her body tighten, then immediately relaxed as her pussy tightened and began throbbing around my fingers

"Oh fuck! Thomas! I'm about to cum! Please do not stop!"

"Yes, babe cum! Let it go. Give me that fucking cum!"

I started to speed as I felt her cum slowly oozing out of her sweetness. Knowing she was cumming all over my dick turn me on more.

"Oh my God! What are you doing to me? I can't stop cumming"

The moment she said that she started to squirt all over my arm and the table. I pulled my finger out of her and she squirted enough on to my shirt to make me smile. I quickly started finger fucking her again. This time with more force and deeper, which only made her cum harder. I pulled my fingers out of her and took a step back and watched her body uncontrollably twitch. She was trying to talk, but she couldn't find the words.

I smiled to myself, walked back over to her, and flipped her over on to her stomach where she would be facing me. I unzipped my pants, and before I had my pants all the way down, she reached out, grabbed my dick, and pulled me closer so she could start sucking me. In no time I had to put my hands on the table to brace myself. When I regained my composure, I reestablished control by grabbing her by her hair and pulling her head back.

"Open your mouth," I instructed her.

Without a single word, she did as she was told, giving me full access to her mouth. I slowly slipped my cock down her throat as deep as I could and held it there.

I could see her eyes start to water, her makeup running down her face. *Go deeper!*

Her nails dug into my skin until my flesh was penetrated. I pulled out of her mouth. I could see a long trail of saliva from her lips to the tip. She had a look of ecstasy on her face, her smile was a devilish smirk, and without warning she shoveled it back down her throat until she made herself choke.

After exiting her mouth I lead her to the kitchen and forcefully turned her around and bent her over the countertop. I grab my dick and lightly rubbed it up and down her soaked pussy lips. Her breathing began to speed up again as she pushed herself back into me trying to slip my dick into her sweetness.

I allowed myself to go halfway inside of her, then pull back until only the tip remained. As I repeat the half stroke I could feel her legs starting to shake, her arms weaken. She turned her head to the side and rested her upper body onto the counter exposing her ass and pussy to me giving me better all access. I sped the pace up going deeper, harder, faster, and with disregard to the pain shooting down my left leg. Her hands balled up into fist as she yelled announcing that she was cumming.
I pumped her hard and deep until I felt her sweet juices running down my leg, soon the moisture of our sex coved us both. I lifted my arm and begun to lick her sweetness.
"Fuck! Thomas! I can't stop cumming."

"This is what you wanted! This is what you said you need…what you crave!"

"Yes! Please give me that big black cock. Fuck your white pussy!"

I slowed the speed down to a slow steady long stroke. I pulled my dick out and smacked her ass. I stood there and watched how her body uncontrollably convulsed. I was barely able to stand. All of her weight was on her arm braced on the grey granite countertops.

"Oh my God, what are you doing to me?"

I smiled, "I'm doing to you exactly what you need and want to be done to you."

I grabbed her by the hand and led her into the master bedroom.

Chapter 13

The lights were off, but in the far corners of the room there were two candles lit. The candles gave me just enough light to see what and where I was going. When I got to the foot of the bed, I turned to face her and as I was turning, she was dropping to her knees to take my hard manhood in her mouth. She was about halfway down before I stopped her and pulled her back up to her feet.

I looked her in her eyes and said, "No! Tonight, is about your pleasure, it not about me."

She looked into my eyes and smiled. I picked her up and gently placed her onto the bed. I lifted her right leg up and delivered gentle kisses on them. I made my way down to her inner thigh. I lifted her leg up higher and started to kiss her calf and then behind her knee. Pushing her leg farther back I made my way down to her outer thigh. I moved her leg over so I could turn her over onto her stomach. She followed my lead and turned over, but instead of laying on her stomach she was on all fours. With the height of the bed her perfect ass was located directly in my face.

I took a half a step forward and kissed her ass cheeks. I started to run my finger up and down both sides of her outer thighs. I reached up and grabbed her ass and started to kiss her all over. I started to plant light kisses on her back. I started at the base of her spine and slowly made my way up.
She shivered and said, "Damn, what are you trying to do to me?"

"I'm doing what you want me to do to you."

She laughed and said, "You say that like I have no choice."

"You do not have a choice."

"I always have a choice."

She grabbed me by the neck, pulled me down, and kissed me so hard I could feel my lips pressing against my teeth. The kiss had meaning and depth to it. I felt as if something was changing. She wrapped her legs around me and reach down and grabbed my dick and slipped it inside of her.
She was so wet, so warm, so tight. It felt as if I was meant to be in that precise spot at that very moment.

I slowly started to slip my dick deeper inside of her. I was as deep as I could get, making sure that I give every inch of her inner walls the attention they desperately needed. After about three full rotations I slowly pulled out until only the very tip is inside of her. I started to slowly insert my cock back inside of her inch by inch. Once I was deep, I repeated the circular motion and pulled back out. When I started to go back inside, she begun to dig her nails into my back thinking she knew what was coming, but I only put maybe half inside of her and sped up the pace. She was trying to pull me in closer so I could go deeper, but I didn't allow her to get any more of me inside of her. She was only going to get what I was going to give her. In due time she would be getting all the dick she could handle.

When I pulled my dick out of her, I looked down to see white cream covering my cock. She saw the same beautiful sight that I saw. She looked at me and smiled and turned over giving me full access to her from behind. I will never get over how beautiful her body was. She looked back at me said, "You like what you see Daddy, because it's all yours."

I couldn't hold back my smile as I slide my rock-hard cock into her wet waiting pussy. I only had the tip in when she started to cum. She pushed back on me and engulfed my entire cock. I put my left hand on the center of her back, with my right hand on the base of her neck and pushed her down onto the bed. I positioned my leg on the outside of her legs. Giving me full control of how much of my cock she was going to get, and she was going to get it all.

Steady paced deep strokes, but I made sure that she didn't get the whole thing until she was cumming all over me. I started to feel her pussy tighten up on my cock and suddenly loosen, and that was the moment I knew she was about ready to explode. I sped up and she started to scream.

"I'm cumming again. Fuck me!"

"I can't hear you! Say it louder."

"Thomas, please fuck me harder!"
"Damm babe you are so fucking wet. Fuck! That pussy is so fucking good."

"Fuck I'm still fucking cumming…please don't stop please! Fuck me harder! Give me all that black cock motherfucker."

I reached back and smacked her ass, "Say please!"

"Please give me that big black cock! Please fuck me until my pussy hurts."

I could feel her squirting all over me and it turned me on more and more. I slowed down and whenever I had most of my cock out her, I would slam it back inside of her, and every time I slammed her, I could feel more of her cum shooting out. I put more of my weight on to her small frame making her flatten out on the bed. This time when I slammed my cock deep inside of her, I started to grind it deeper in her. The deeper I

went the harder she came. The more she came the harder I went. The more she came the more turned on I became. The more turn on I became the deeper and faster I went. I got to a pace that surprised me. I looked down at her and her body became limp, so I slowed down and leaned in to see her face to make sure she was okay, but to my pure delight her eyes were wide open staring off into the distance with a smile on her face
I wasn't finish with her just yet.

I turned her to her side and pushed her leg up to her chest and slipped my hard cum covered cock back into her again. When I started to fuck her again her eyes widened and looked at me. She had no more to give. I smiled at her because I had a little more.

I put the tip of my dick to the sweet opening of her wetness and it slipped right in because how wet she was. *Wow!* I started fucking her again at a very rapid pace. She grabbed my hands and put them on her neck, and I did what she asked and started to squeeze. A few seconds later she yelled that she was about to cum and for me to fuck her harder. Her eyes rolled behind her head. The closer I got to cumming the faster I went.

"Fuck babe! Cum for me babe!"

"You want that cum.!

"Please give it to me babe, please!"

"Where do you want it babe. Tell me where you want it."

"Inside of me! Fill me! Please fill me with your cum."

When I came it was the most intense orgasm I have ever had in my life. It was like my whole body came. I collapsed on top of her and she pulled me in closer, deeper. She wanted to make sure I was totally drained.

We laid there for a few hours talking about life and the things that we wanted to accomplish, and different bucket list things we wanted to check off. She was telling me that she was first in her class and scored the highest scores in the history of the FBI. Out of nowhere her phone rung, breaking the peaceful flow of our conversation, and brought us back to reality.

"Hello, Agent Green," she said.

I could hardly hear the voice on the other end of the phone giving her an address. He also said we had two more bodies.

Her eyes widen and she said with venom, "We will get this motherfucker. I'm leaving now text me the address."

She looked at me and said, "Babe I have to go."

She had a text message come in on her phone and when she looked down at it, I caught a quick glance, and my heart dropped to the ground. I repeated the text in my head, *456 Hacksaw Trail, 15th floor, Apartment 1502.*

I watched her leave the room and seconds later I heard the door closed. I rolled over and thought about what she was about to find. I knew exactly what she had ahead of her.

I thought about that night and how fast it got out of control, but it was like something in me changed that night and I had no regrets. I just sat there and smiled to myself.

Chapter 14

I reached over and grabbed my belt and wrapped it around her neck and pulled it, cutting off her air. The image of that murderous night popped into my head and I lost myself in what had happened. I pulled out of her and walked over to her bag. I retrieved a black leather paddle with small holes drilled through it. It looked brand new with that new leather smell to it. The handle was wrapped like a baseball bat, but it had leather strips hanging from the end of it.

I knew that I had no good intention with this. I was getting ready to walk back over to the chairs when I saw what looked like a large rubber ball in the corner of the bag. I reach in and pulled out two ball gags and my mind went crazy. I just could not stop thinking about that night, my blood started to flow. I could feel the sweat on my forehead starting to form. My eyes started to water uncontrollably. My body was cold to the touch, but I was hot. The pleasure I was feeling started to take over just at the thought of that night.

I walked behind the Spanish female and started to fuck her hard and fast. I pulled out again and reach to my side to grab the leather paddle. I smacked her ass, not too hard, but not too light either. She looked at me asked was that all I had. I grabbed the ball gag out of the chair and strapped it around her and her friends face to keep them from getting too loud. I walked back over and repositioned myself behind the Spanish girl.

I had the black leather paddle in my hand and without warning I hit her with the paddle. I hit her hard enough to move the table. Tears instantly start to flow from her eyes.

I hit her again and again.

The pleasure I was getting from the power was taking over my judgement. I looked into her friend's eyes and it was pure fear. The lust and pleasure were long gone, but the pleasure I was feeling was so much stronger than anything sex could bring me. It was the feeling of power; unmatched power and I was starving for it.

I walked to the side of the table and grabbed the belt that was still around the white girl's neck to tighten the belt and locked it in. She started fighting to get air, her eyes begging for help. I looked at her and turned and walked away without giving it a second thought.

Next I walked over to the couch and got dressed, then I made my way over and grabbed a chair and sat down at the table. The Spanish girl was in tears and her friend was slowly slipping into a permanent state of darkness.

About the Author...

Rodney Billingsley is the author behind the pen name, Thomas Long. Rodney's life is filled with experiences that drive his passion, and storytelling.

He is a 40-year-old father of two beautiful kids who loves to cook and cater small events. Outside activities are his favorite past time, mostly softball, hiking, and travelling.

In 1998, at the age of 18, he joined the Armed Forces. He completed his military career with an honorable discharge in 2001. Shortly thereafter, a severe back injury required a major surgery. The procedure was a success but within a month, Rodney was addicted to his pain medication, which in hindsight, was the beginning of his downward spiral. This habit evolved from using to selling pain medication then selling even harder drugs.

Rodney was ultimately arrested and sentenced to 3 years in prison with 7 years of probation. Since his release, he has re-entered society as an upstanding citizen with an amazing story to tell.

Thomas Long is just getting started...

Follow the Author

FB: Thomas Long
IG: unexpected_night_2020
Twitter: @ThomasL50407493
unexpectednight.com